I Stood, Filled with Fear

"They took the pets," I said. That's when I realized what had happened: we'd been abandoned. At that moment I discovered what forlorn means. "We've got to get out of here!" I said urgently. "Federation agents could come barging in any minute." I grabbed my daypack and we left, Deneen trotting after me.

Near the middle of the old field was a big corrugated iron shed, built there by the previous owner to house farm machinery. The shed, well out of sight from any public road, was plenty big enough to conceal the old space cutter—the one we'd come in to Evdash.

Sure enough, the cutter was open, waiting for us and already turned on. Dad's voice came from the computer's speaker. "By the time you hear this, your mother and I will be outsystem at warp speed. We hate to leave you, but we have no choice."

FANGLITH

JOHN DALMAS

BAEN
science fiction
BOOKS

FANGLITH

Copyright © 1985 by John Dalmas

A Baen Book

Baen Enterprises
8-10 W. 36th Street
New York, N.Y. 10018

First printing, October 1985

ISBN: 0-671-55988-5

Cover art by Kevin Johnson

Printed in the United States of America

Distributed by
SIMON & SCHUSTER
MASS MERCHANDISE SALES COMPANY
1230 Avenue of the Americas
New York, N.Y. 10020

Dedicated with love to
GAIL,
JUDY,
JACK,
IAN,
JILL,
&
RYAN,
who in that order
came into my life.

ONE

My name is Larn, and because it was my name day, I hadn't had to go to school. Instead I'd gone hiking, with a little fishing thrown in.

A name day, in case they don't have them where you are, is— Well, each day of the year has one or more person's names assigned to it. The day your name falls on is special for you. You get presents, and the day off from school. My major present had been a fishing gun—a small belt model that can shoot a lure out as far as eighty feet.

I didn't realize how special, or what kind of special, this name day was going to be for me.

Actually, when I was born they'd named me Lanar, Lanar kel Deroop, but that was before we came to Evdash. On Evdash we took the name "Rostik." And Larn can be either a given name or, on Evdash, a nickname for Lanar, so I'm known as Larn Rostik.

1

There's a reason for the name changing. I was born on Morn Gebleu, about 1,100 parsecs* away. But after we ran away to Evdash—I was four years old then—our whole family took Evdashian names.

And as soon as we all learned to speak Evdashian without an accent—the languages are really pretty much alike, especially in writing—we moved to a different district and changed our names again. There we pretended we'd always lived on Evdash.

The false birth records, identification documents, and things like that were expensive, but dad didn't want us known as Federation refugees. There was always a chance that Federation agents would come looking for him. His family had been prominent in Federation politics and government for generations. Then, when he was eleven, the Glondis Party took over the government and forced through a bunch of what they called "constitutional reforms," which meant they canceled a lot of the people's rights.

So he'd studied business instead of government, with a lot of science on the side.

When he was twenty-five, the Glondisans threw out the constitution entirely and did whatever they pleased, which meant putting people they didn't like in jail. And there were a lot of people they didn't like.

---

*A parsec is a unit of distance 3.258 light years long, or 19.18 trillion miles. Units of measurement, such as years and miles, are ordinarily given here in Earth equivalents instead of Standard.

Then dad became a leader in an underground group that published an illegal newspaper. I've always suspected that he and mom had done other underground stuff, too, that they never mentioned to us. Anyway, he bought a used space cutter, which was illegal. He also bought a whole data cube on habitable planets outside the Federation—old colonies, a lot of them. Then he loaded us all in and took off for Evdash.

It was pretty risky, of course, what with the patrol ships around Morn Gebleu, and pursuit ships ready to scramble and lock course with any fugitive. But my baby sister Deneen and I didn't know that. I was busy with my box of toy space marines, while Deneen was into stuffed animals, as I recall.

So almost all of my memories were of Evdash, almost three hundred parsecs outside the Federation boundary.

Anyway, this was my name day, and I came out of the hayfield behind our house carrying a couple of fish on a stringer—a long twig of brush with the side twigs trimmed off. I noticed that the family floater wasn't parked on its pad by the back door, but that didn't mean anything to me. Dad might have gone to see a client (he was a business consultant) or mom could have flown into town to shop.

Actually I was thinking about how we were going to wipe the field with Welser Academy in our banner game the next day. I was the goalie, with the quickest moves in the district.

I went into the house through the utility room, hanging my daypack on its hook and dumping my fish in the utility sink. I figured to clean them after I'd had a cold drink.

"Hi!" I called when I went into the kitchen. No one answered, so I assumed that mom and dad had left together. I opened the fridge to take out the margel pitcher, and the pitcher wasn't there. It was in the sink, empty. Now *that* got my attention. First of all I wanted some, and there wasn't any. Also, our family has certain agreed-upon rules, and each of us takes responsibility for them. Whoever uses the margel down to below the cup mark mixes a new batch, puts ice in it, and puts it back in the fridge. Deneen and I rarely forget, and besides, we'd been away all day. And I could hardly imagine mom or dad forgetting.

I mixed a new batch, had some on ice, then went into dad's office. He often leaves a message on his computer screen when he goes out. And there was the second strange thing—the computer was off line! It's usually left on continuously unless we leave for several days.

Somehow I felt strange about that—goose-pimply strange. I invoked it and asked if there was any message. It didn't seem to understand, so I switched to keyboard memory—still nothing. It was completely erased except for the basic, built-in functions! Then I yanked open the cabinet door, and all the program and data cubes were gone!

Now *that* made my hair stand on end! It was totally crazy. And what popped into my head was Federation agents. Dad and mom were both gone; they'd left deliberately and didn't expect to come back. And dad had wiped the computer and taken or destroyed the cubes so agents couldn't learn anything.

And where did that leave me?

I started to look around for a written message, then realized that didn't make any sense. If they'd expected agents to come along before I got home, they wouldn't leave a message that agents could read.

About that time I heard the front door and almost had heart failure. But then my sister's voice called out. "Hi, everybody, I'm home!" I went into the living room just in time to see her start to tell someone's number to the vid. I lunged at the manual *off* button. She stared at me like I was a lunatic.

"What," she challenged, "is *that* all about? I'm supposed to call Narni when I get home from school today."

"Something's happened," I said, "something serious. We can't use the vid."

For a 14-year-old sister, she was pretty easy to get along with, compared to lots of guys' sisters. Dad and mom didn't mind it when we argued about something real, up to a point. But since they wouldn't tolerate either of us sniping at the other, we hadn't developed a big brother-sister hostility. So when I said that something serious had happened, her expression went from irritation to skeptical interest. I told her what I'd found and what I'd figured out as the reason.

"The agents may have our channel tapped and be monitoring our phone," I concluded.

"Federation agents?" she said. "There's got to be a less dramatic reason than that." Then, before I could say "such as what?", she turned and walked rapidly into our parents' bedroom. I hurried behind her, wondering what she was doing.

What we found was that their closets were about thirty percent cleaned out. All their rougher clothes, boots, and sport shoes were gone. A few things were even on the floor, as if they'd just grabbed stuff and run! I got the notion they'd scattered them on purpose, to make sure we would realize that something had happened.

Then Deneen went to her own room, again with me trotting along behind. Her closet was in the same shape as theirs. When I saw that, I realized what she'd been thinking, and hurried off to look in my own closet. The only difference was that they hadn't taken as much from ours, and had left the stuff we liked best.

"You're right," she said, "and they wanted it to look as if we'd all left. Have you seen Cookie?"

That clinched it. Cookie is our house felid— about twenty pounds of altered, overweight kitty. He was too lazy to go any farther than his "garden patch" behind the house, where he went to poop and pee. He could be depended on to nag you for a snack if he'd been left alone, but I hadn't seen or heard a thing from him. So he was gone, too.

I shook my head. "They took the pets," I said. That's when I really realized what had happened: we'd been abandoned! At that moment I discovered what *forlorn* means. The key things that made life seem safe and predictable and pleasant were gone.

But we didn't have time for a pity party,

because then it hit me. "We've got to get out of here!" I said urgently. "Agents could come barging in any minute."

"What makes you think they haven't been here already, and gone?" Deneen said reasonably.

I hadn't thought of that. "Maybe they have, maybe they haven't. We'd better get out anyway. They might come back, you know."

We started for the back door. I'd just opened it when she stopped by the utility sink. "Are you going to leave those there?" she asked, pointing to my fish.

That would be dumb, all right. The fish were too fresh. And if agents had been there and came back, they'd know for sure that one or more of us were still around, collectible. Muttering to myself, I shoved the fish and the stringer into the composter and flushed them through. Then I trotted back into the kitchen, washed the contents of the margel pitcher down the drain, and left it in the sink where I'd found it. Then I ran back into dad's office and turned off the computer again. Finally, I grabbed my daypack off the hook and we left, Deneen trotting after me to the barn.

"Why the barn?" she asked.

"We can sit in the cupola and talk—figure things out. We've got to decide what to do."

We climbed the ladder into the hayloft, then another into the cupola that stood like a stubby little tower above the barn roof. Three or four years earlier, I'd nailed a stout plank up there to sit on, like a bench, and we sat down on it. No one could see us up there, but we could see out in any direction. The cupola had been built to ventilate the hayloft. Each of its four sides consisted of a louver, with down-slanting slats that let air between them freely but kept rain from coming in and wetting the hay. We could see at an angle downward—see the ground for a couple of hundred feet around.

"Any bright ideas?" Deneen asked.

"Just questions, for now. First of all, where did they go? Are they apt to come back looking for us in a day or so, when the agents have had time to leave? Have they left Evdash completely, or are they somewhere fifty miles away?"

"Off-planet," she answered without hesitating. "Obviously." Then, seeing that it wasn't obvious to me at all, she went on. "The only way Federation agents could have found us was if someone informed on us. Apparently someone took the time and expense to go back to the Federation and tell. So if dad and mom came back here again, the same someone would probably know. Dad would have figured that out."

"They could come back, pick us up, and take off again. There's no reason that wouldn't work."

She shrugged.

"What I'm trying to figure out," I said, "is, do we stay put or go off somewhere? If we stay here, we'll have to keep hidden, or the informer might find out we're still around. And when we don't show up at school tomorrow, someone is apt to come around to ask questions when they don't get anyone on the vid. They're sure to within a couple of days.

The sheriff could even have men out here looking around in a day or so."

Deneen frowned. "Maybe when it gets dark," she said, "we should walk to the Carlinton aerospace port and see if the cutter's still there. If it is, they haven't left the planet. They're still around somewhere."

"They could have used the old cutter we came from Morn Gebleu in," I said. "It's closer. And as far as I know, it's still operational. I never heard dad say it's not."

"I doubt if it is, though," said Deneen. "Otherwise, why would they have bought a new one?"

"Because they didn't want anyone to know we had a Federation-built cutter. That would really mark us as foreigners. And remember how sneaky dad was, bringing it here late at night? Maybe we'd better check it out before we walk six miles to Carlinton."

I'd just said it when a floater came curving smoothly in, looking just like ours. For a second I had this thought that it was mom and dad, and they were coming home from somewhere. That there was another totally different, ordinary explanation for everything, and we were all going to have a big laugh over how worried I'd been.

But it wasn't ours. When it slipped onto the parking pad beside the house, we could see *Budget Rental* on the side. Three men got out and went in the house without knocking. They were inside for about twenty minutes. When they came out, they stood by the floater for a minute or two, talking. They were only about seventy or eighty feet from us, and not trying to be quiet, so we could hear pretty much everything they said.

"No, they've left for Fanglith," said one of them. "Somebody warned him. That's the only explanation."

"If he was warned, maybe he also knows we know about Fanglith," said another.

"I doubt it. What *I'd* like to know is how he knew we were coming."

"Maybe he didn't," said the third. "Maybe he just happened to leave today. Maybe he'll be back."

"He took his cutter, didn't he? Use your head, Talley! Grabbed his family and some clothes, his data cubes, left the power on, food in the fridge, and took off. Probably for Fanglith. Let's get going. We'll report to the captain and see what he wants to do. He'll probably have to go to Corlus Base for orders."

They got back in their floater and left. Deneen and I looked at each other. "Thanks," I said to her.

"For what?"

"For reminding me about those fish."

She nodded. "That's all right, Larn," she said. "We're even. Thanks for spotting that something was wrong and realizing what it was." She looked at me. She's really got direct eyes, and no flinch at all that I ever noticed. "It hasn't always been easy," she went on, "being the little sister of the smartest kid in school. Sometimes I've tried to cut you down a notch, which is not all right, but just now I'm glad you're a hotshot."

"Me?" I said. That surprised heck out of me. Intellectually I've always been aware that

I'm pretty darn good. But at an emotional level—the level of *feelings*—I've often felt like a bit of a dummy. As if the appearance of being smart and able was false—that I was really not all that good. And I'd always felt like she could see through me.

"Huh!" I said, "it never occurred to me that you thought I was all that smart. I've always thought *you* were the smart one. Dad said once, when you were maybe eleven or twelve, that you had the eye and the analytical mind of a stress engineer or a tax lawyer, he wasn't sure which."

She grinned at me for a moment—I'm not sure I'd ever seen her look just like that before—then sobered. "We'd better be smart," she said, "because we've got a problem."

It struck me right then that while we had a problem all right, I wasn't really worried. The forlorn feeling was gone, and somehow it seemed to me at that moment that everything would work out just fine.

But before I could say so, we heard a "woof!" It was outside the barn, and it could only be Bubba, our family canid. Deneen and I looked at each other, then scrambled down out of the cupola and then the hayloft. It was Bubba, all right, all 120 rock-hard pounds of him. Either our parents hadn't taken him with them, or they were hiding out somewhere nearby and had sent him to get us.

Bubba read my thoughts on that, of course. He's an espwolf—one of the telepathic canids of a backwater world on the far side of the Federation. Life on their planet got more or less wiped out by a collision with some large wandering asteroid, but the pioneer colonists there got off ahead of it and took some of the espwolves with them. Dad says there are a few breeding pairs around, back on Morn Gebleu.

You can't own an espwolf, or you didn't used to be able to, because they're sophonts—they have intelligence like people, more or less. It's hard to say if they're *fully* as intelligent as human beings, because they're quite a lot different. I'm sure that Bubba is smarter than lots of people; he's more *sensible* than most of them. But his mental processes seem to be simpler. He's usually not much for planning, but he takes quick logical actions.

But while you can't own an espwolf, if you're lucky, you can make a working arrangement with one of them. If one of them likes you, and you like him or her, then he or she can become part of your family. On their own planet, they lived and hunted in packs, which are extended families, and they really aren't ever very happy unless they're part of a family. So if you're a bachelor, forget it. They're not interested in families that small, except maybe as a temporary arrangement, I suppose.

Anyway, when we came down out of the hayloft, Bubba said, "Dad and mom gone to sky. Me take Larn and Deneen somewhere for dad. Come!" And with that he trotted out of the yard and started across the hayfield, Deneen and I trailing behind.

Now it's not that he said it just like that, but he really does talk. First of all, he can read our minds but we can't read his. And his mouth and throat weren't designed for .human speech. So being both logical and telepathic, he'd come up with a system of his own sounds to talk to us with. Actually, in a way, he uses Evdashian words, but substitutes sounds he can make in place of the Evdashian sounds, and our family can understand whatever he says.

Getting out the necessary *variety* of sounds is awkward for a wolf's mouth, of course, so he doesn't talk more than he has to, and leaves out words he doesn't need, but he has a good enough vocabulary.

Anyway, it's a good relationship, with respect and affection both ways. We like and admire him and he feels the same toward us.

One thing for sure, he could run a lot faster than we could. He crossed the hayfield at, for him, an easy trot, but it had me breathing hard and deep. Deneen was really puffing. Her sports are gymnastics and, privately, martial arts, not cross-country. Back of the hayfield was a big woods of large old trees that connected up with the river forest. When we got to it, out of sight of any possible floater that might fly over, Bubba slowed up a little but still kept trotting.

Back of the woods was a big abandoned field, growing up with thorny bushes and lots of tree saplings. In another ten or fifteen years it would be a young woods. When we came to it and Bubba kept going straight, I realized where he was taking us.

Near the middle of the old field was a big corrugated iron shed that had been built there by the previous owner to house farm machinery. That was one reason dad had bought this particular place. This old shed, well out of sight of any public road, was plenty big enough to conceal the old space cutter—the one we'd come in to Evdash.

Only the shed would be locked and so would the cutter; I'd have to go back and see if I could find the key. But Bubba knew what I was thinking, and woofed, "No, it okay," so I kept trotting along behind him. And sure enough, the shed was unlocked and the cutter was open, waiting for us.

Inside the cutter, Bubba stood on his hind legs with his somewhat handlike front paws by the computer. It was already turned on. "Push Bubba," he said.

For a moment I didn't understand what he meant, then typed B-U-B-B-A on the keyboard. Dad's and mom's faces appeared on the screen.

Dad's voice came from the computer's speaker. "So far, so good," he said. "By the time you see this, your mother and I will be outsystem at warp speed. We hate to leave you, but we have no choice. Not long after you left this morning, we were warned that a Federation police corvette had been intercepted and boarded by an Evdashian picket cruiser. The corvette's captain showed a warrant for our arrest, and apparently either a bribe was passed, or more probably a Federation military threat. At any rate, they were given permission to land agents, although their warrant didn't have any authority on Evdash.

"They had our address. I'm sure my informant intended to delay them as much as he could without being obvious about it, but at best, we didn't have much time."

That's how the message started. They left Bubba to see that we got it. They'd only be gone for a few months—a year, at most. Long enough to decide where to settle next. Then they'd come back and get us. They'd planned earlier for the possibility that something like this might happen, he went on. Dad had set up a bank account for us in another town, and had also arranged for us to live with a family there, under assumed names.

But Deneen and I had information that mom and dad didn't seem to: Not only had someone leaked where we lived to the Federation government, but the government thought they knew where dad and mom might go from here.

And would the leak also know about this new family? Maybe the new family *was* the leak. Deneen and I talked it over, Bubba sitting on the deck with his knowing eyes moving from one to the other of us as we talked.

Deneen put her finger on the real situation, though. If the political police thought they knew where mom and dad were going, then presumably they'd follow them there—to Fanglith, wherever that was.

Neither of us had ever heard of Fanglith.

I looked the computer over. It didn't look much different from those that Deneen and I were familiar with, and presumably it worked about the same. I mean, computers have been computers since before the historical era. They didn't invent them independently on Evdash. The colonists had brought them with them from the Federation a few centuries ago, back when the Federation was the Borgreen Empire.

There was a key marked *ops ind*—that should be operations index. I touched it and a series of operating instructions rolled slowly up the screen. In half a minute I had accessed the information on Fanglith, what information there was. It was obviously on a contraband data cube because the data wasn't preceded by an approval code.

Fanglith, it said, was a planet, perhaps fictitious, supposed to have been known from the legendary Ninth Dynasty. About 18,000 years before the historical era, it was supposedly used as a prison planet by the legendary mad Emperor Karkzhuk, founder of the Bloody Dynasty. In fact, the word *fanglith* was supposed to have meant *prison* in the slang of that time.

Karkzhuk was said to have rounded up several thousand writers, artists, actors, and others who had satirized his government or offended him in some way or other. He also supposedly arrested a number of key political activists, and scientists accused of doing research on unapproved subjects. They were all mindwiped, according to the story, put on an imperial troop transport, shipped to the uninhabited planet Fanglith, and just dumped there—left on the surface with nothing, not even clothes. Not even memory.

The information on Fanglith referred to the Ninth Dynasty survey records. The computer index listed two cubes that had something to say about them. One was a standard encyclopedia entry. The other was a contraband data

cube. I accessed the encyclopedia entry first.
It was pretty interesting.

There may or may not have been an actual
Ninth Dynasty, but there definitely seems to
have been a survey made earlier than 24,000
years ago. Supposedly, it listed hundreds of
habitable planets outside the empire, now the
Federation. But it had been lost before the
beginning of the historical era, which started
5,213 standard years ago. All that was left of
it now were jealously guarded copies of copies of individual sectors that various merchant
explorers, adventurers, and pirates had been
interested in at one time or another. Fakes
had also been made to sell to them, and most
of the existing copies were thought to be fakes.
The planets listed on most of them were
imaginary.

But some of the copies were real. During
recorded history, re-exploration in some sectors showed that the worlds described on certain copies actually existed.

After that I accessed the contraband data
cube and asked the computer for its data on
Fanglith. All we got was a set of time-corrected
galactic coordinates—the designation of a uni-
formly moving point in space—and a few
words I couldn't read. Real or phony? I had
no idea.

"I'll bet Fanglith is for real," Deneen said
as we stared at the figures. "I'll bet something's going on there. Maybe it's a staging
world for rebel activities against the Federation!"

I raised an eyebrow. "Unlikely," I said, shaking off the spell of the coordinates. "Fanglith

is supposed to be way farther out than this."
My fingers touched some keys, and the figures
appeared on the screen. "It's more than 700
parsecs outside the Federation border zone!
There's got to be a hundred million star systems outside the Federation that are within
700 parsecs. The odds that the survey found
and looked over planets that far out has got to
be close to zero."

While I was saying this, I'd instructed the
computer to tell us how far from Evdash the
supposed coordinates for Fanglith were. In
round numbers it was 646 parsecs.

"Why would dad buy the cube if he didn't
think it was any good?" Deneen asked reasonably. She has this talent for looking past details and grabbing key points. "And apparently
he talked about Fanglith to someone, probably the informer. Anyway, the political police
seem to believe in it."

"You know what dad says about the political police," I answered. "They love rumors.
He might have started one about Fanglith himself, just to throw them off."

"Um-hm," she said thoughtfully. "Or maybe
he didn't. Maybe Fanglith is out there, right
where those coordinates say it is. And maybe
he and mom are on their way there right now.
I'll bet the Federation corvette will probably
get orders at Corlus Base to go there and hunt
for them. And they won't even know it unless
we tell them.

"We've got the coordinates," she went on,
"and Fanglith is either there or it's not. If the
flight and life support systems on this cutter
are okay for a two-month flight, or however

long it is, we'd better go out there and check before the police do."

She turned to Bubba then. "You've been awfully quiet. What do you say? Were mom and dad going to Fanglith?"

As usual, Bubba was as direct as Deneen. "Don't know. They going somewhere, not think name while I with them. We go find out."

"Okay, you guys," I said, "let's see if this thing can make the trip." I keyed in the ops index again and found out how to call up a status report on the ship's systems, including life support. All systems were operational. The fuel slugs were no problem, of course; they'd outlast the cutter. It took a couple of minutes to get an analysis on existing food stores and water quality, but they were okay, too. And the supplies were plentiful, as though dad had replenished them before he put the cutter in storage.

"You guys realize," I said, "that once we get there, if there is such a world, our job has just started. Unless it *is* a staging planet with a big rebel base. And we don't even know there are organized rebels anywhere nowadays. Can you imagine hunting for a 24-foot cutter down somewhere, no one knows where, on a wild planet?"

"What makes you think it's wild?" Deneen asked.

"There was no one there at all 23,000 years ago. Then they took a few thousand people there, so the story goes, *mindwiped* yet, so they didn't remember anything. They must have been like a bunch of confused apes. There was no one there to help them get started—no tools, no fire, nothing.

"Probably most of them died the first year, so maybe there were a few hundred to carry on from there. They'd look up at the stars and wonder what those were. They'd see a little fire from a lightning strike and probably run away from it.

"I hope to heck it is a staging planet, because otherwise I don't see how we'll ever find them."

"We've got Bubba," Deneen said reasonably.

I'd entirely overlooked that! I've read that epswolves can find packmates telepathically at distances up to fifty miles, so we had a parent-detector! Things suddenly began to look more hopeful. If Fanglith would just be there!

We tried to think of everything we needed to consider before leaving, and it looked perfectly feasible to do it. With a cutter, the trip was no big deal except for the time it would take. You could go to any set of galactic coordinates. The problem was that not one set in trillions was close to a star system, let alone to a planet.

Bubba wasn't worried, though. He thought the trip was a great idea. He didn't say anything, but his tongue was hanging halfway to the deck from his grinning mouth.

We did need more clothes, so Deneen and I jogged home, leaving Bubba to guard the cutter. We also got our lightweight sleeping bags, and stuffed our trek packs with everything we thought we might need. We didn't know what to expect—deserts, swamps, icy mountains, or what. Maybe some of each. When we left the house, we not only carried our packs, but a big pillowcase each, filled with stuff.

Back at the machine shed, it was all the two of us together could do to push the big machine doors open so we could get the cutter out. They were designed to be opened by hand all right, but they acted as if the running wheels had corroded in the track. But finally they gave, and we got them open enough that the cutter would fit through.

That's when I discovered that the operating instructions said nothing about handling in and out of small openings. It didn't have the same kind of controls that a floater does, and I had no experience at all with it. So I had Deneen raise it a foot or so above the dirt floor and I got out and pushed. In a couple of minutes the cutter was outside.

It was starting to get dark then, and in the gathering dusk I keyed in our destination— Fanglith—and the Standard date to the nearest minute, of course, assuming our watches were right. That would continually correct the coordinates to present time.

Deneen looked pretty serious, and Bubba wasn't grinning as big as he had been. I closed the *go* switch, and the cutter began to rise, accelerating smoothly, the computer in charge now.

We were on our way to a world whose name meant prison, or maybe to no world at all.

TWO

We spent somewhat more than an hour in mass proximity phase. It was a strange hour— that is, it felt strange. Strange to be leaving Evdash, the only home either of us could really remember, without parents or friends, and going someplace neither of us knew anything about. If I'd read about something like that, I'd have thought it was neat—an adventure. And it was an adventure, as far as that was concerned. But it didn't feel that neat. Some friendly author hadn't plotted out ahead how we'd get safely through all the dangers and uncertainties and come out wise and winning. It was all on us to make it come out right. Or maybe to end up squashed one way or another. For sure, the odds looked pretty darned poor that we'd find our parents.

Even Deneen was looking sober. We sat in the control room, which was also the living room and eating room, watching through the big wraparound window. For a while we could see Donia, Evdash's major moon, as we drew up on it and passed it at something like sixty or eighty thousand miles to our right.

After Donia fell behind, we just watched the stars. We knew that when we went into FTL mode, we wouldn't have anything at all to watch outside the cutter until we arrived in Fanglith's star system. There'd be just the three of us, in one small cutter, for 57 standard days, with who knew what at the other end.

Finally, the cutter's navigational instruments determined that we were far enough from Evdash's gravitational field, and that was it. It transferred into faster-than-light mode and jumped. After that there was only blackness to see outside, with no stars visible.

Soon after that, Deneen said she was going to bed, and left the control room. Bubba had already gone to sleep there on the deck, with his chin between his paws. But me, old Larn the worrier, I wasn't sleepy. So I browsed through the library index of the computer, flagging for quick access, entries that looked interesting. If Fanglith was as primitive as I expected, I wanted to know something about primitive worlds.

There aren't any primitive human worlds in the Federation, of course, or any known outside the Federation. There hadn't been any since long before the historical era. But some of the felid worlds had been studied and described while they were still primitive, and we could read about them. Basically, civilized felids aren't a whole lot different from humans in the ways they think and act. I could hope that if Fanglith was primitive, it wouldn't be too different from some of the felid worlds were when they had been primitive.

We were lucky that dad had stocked the computer with a good library. Both he and mom were action-type people—doers, not simply "readers about." But they both were also interested in the universe and in life around them, and they liked to *know* things, so they read a lot, too.

Still, after about thirty days, I'd had my fill of reading about primitive felid societies. It's not that they weren't interesting; they were. But I'd overstuffed myself. I knew about the clans and septs of the Lake District of Moviru, chivalry among the nobility of Grounia, ship-building on Faswaur, and the construction and uses of steam engines on Maya Worawi, among other things. I'd even learned a bunch of really interesting stuff about superstitions and mysticism among the striped urso-felids of the ringed planet Fylvikh.

I didn't know then whether any of this made me any better prepared to get along on Fanglith or not. Actually, I don't think I'd have lasted a day on Fanglith without it.

When we'd read everything we could find on primitive felid worlds, we started browsing through anything else that looked interesting. Both of us also got so we slept more and more, as though we were trying to hibernate away the monotony of the trip. Of course, Bubba had been sleeping a lot from the beginning. And we started exercising to keep from getting too soft; we might need our muscles when we got there. Deneen began experimenting in the little galley, too, and taught me to bake bread and stuff.

But we were getting pretty impatient to arrive at Fanglith, whatever we found there.

THREE

After fifty-seven days, it was really good to get out of FTL mode. We could look out the window and actually see something, including a planet that looked bigger and bigger as we approached it.

I could remember when I was four, and we had come out of FTL. Mom had wakened us kids and brought us into the control room to show us Evdash as a blue and white three-quarter sphere on the viewscreen. The planet we were approaching now looked just about like it. It was neat to see. Planets like that—human-habitable—are scattered really thinly in this galaxy. And I guess that mankind, having been a spacefaring species for tens of thousands of years, has developed some kind of genetic imprint of real pleasure at the sight of one hanging nearby in space.

I know that Mr. Heggens, our biology teacher, would say "flunk!" at something like that,

26

and tell me I was thinking teleologically. But Mr. Heggens never had an idea of his own in his whole life, and he'd never been in space. If it wasn't in a textbook, for him it wasn't true, and it shouldn't be true for anyone else, either.

During several swings around the planet, broad-band radio scanning brought us no signals of human origin on or around this world, so I figured there weren't any picket ships on patrol and almost certainly no radio broadcasts on the surface. But here was what looked like a human-habitable planet right where the navigation program said Fanglith was supposed to be, give or take a few million miles, so we decided it had to be Fanglith.

I moved in closer on the nightside, looking for the lights of cities, and got nothing. That fitted my idea that any people there would be primitive. We spent most of the next three Standard days flying two miles above the local surface, following the dayside around the planet on a systematic line survey of continents and major islands. "Human-habitable" didn't necessarily mean that it actually had people on it, or that you could land anywhere and there they'd be. We needed to find them.

Deneen and I took turns standing six-hour watches, which made it a long three days. Most of Fanglith had no people at all, or at least so few that we didn't see any sign of them, particularly in the big equatorial jungles and the subarctic forests. But some areas had quite a lot of humans, with farms, scattered villages, and even an occasional town. We saw a couple of places big enough to call cities, but even they probably didn't have more than fifty or maybe a hundred thousand people each. They were seaports, with a bunch of crude little sailing ships and ships that traveled around using long oars.

There must have been a few other cities, too, that we didn't see. But on Fanglith, most people, almost all of them, lived out in the country.

At lots of places we stopped for a few minutes and looked things over under high magnification. Almost everything bigger than a village had a defensive wall around it, sometimes made of stone and sometimes only a stockade, maybe surrounded by a ditch. Even some of the villages had stockades around them.

Besides which, there were a lot of forts and castles scattered around, some of them large. But most were small, with a single big house and a few sheds and barns, surrounded by a wall of one kind or another. If the area had quite a bit of forest, the main building was usually of timber, and the wall or walls were usually a palisade of upright logs, or sometimes two palisades. If there wasn't much forest around, the forts were usually farther apart and made of stone. Some of the stone forts were big, and some only amounted to one small stone tower.

Sometimes we'd see a fort or castle in a district that hardly seemed to have any people at all in it, and some of them looked like they weren't used any longer. A lot of the men wore steel caps, and some wore a kind of coat that looked like metal fish scales and had to be armor. Quite a few carried bows, and others had spears. Almost all that seemed to be warriors of any kind wore swords.

We were glad we'd studied the material about the primitive felid societies. Otherwise, we wouldn't even have known what we were looking at—what a bow was for, or a castle—although I suppose we would have figured most of it out, or found out, if we'd lived long enough.

Something else the felid worlds gave us was a frame of social reference—something to judge what the people were like down there. They were *dangerous*, we both agreed on that.

We certainly didn't see any sign of a rebel staging area, so we had to abandon any real hope of that. There wasn't any indication, visual or instrumental, of power convertors, energy weapons, or even atmospheric flying craft. In fact, we didn't even see any primitive steam-powered machinery. With the exception of ships' sails or an occasional waterwheel, everything seemed to be powered by muscles—animal or human.

Some of the felid planets had been this primitive, while others had used steam for power, or internal combustion engines, or atomic fusion. But human civilization had had power convertors and the space distortion drive for probably 30,000 years, at least. Tradition said a lot longer than that; how much longer depended on which tradition. But anyway, there weren't any known human worlds that were primitive—except, now, this one.

Some, like Evdash, had certain more or less primitive practices. But that was a matter of public or private choice or local economics.

Fanglith was probably the only human world that didn't use power convertors and the space drive, so it looked as if the story of Emperor Karkzhuk and his prison planet were real instead of myth. We were looking at the evidence.

The most impressive single thing we saw, those three days, was a battle. If we'd had any doubt that this was a warlike world, the battle settled it. We were flying over a sort of semidesert when we noticed two dust clouds, so we detoured to see what was making them. It was two armies of cavalry, with thousands of men in each. The animals they rode on were the standard Fanglith riding animal, which is a lot like a gorn.

And there wasn't any question about it—they were getting ready to fight each other. We sat at about one and a half miles elevation, off to one side so we could see the whole panorama through the wraparound window, and the viewscreen could be adjusted to give us a close-up of men fighting, anywhere in the battle that we wanted.

It might sound kind of bloodthirsty to sit up there and watch real live people chop each other up as if they were in some kind of wild holodrama. But they were going to do it anyway, and it seemed to us that we might as well know what war was like on Fanglith.

In one of the armies the men wore robes, although they may have worn armor underneath. In the other army they wore jacket armor that seemed to be made of small metal plates. After a little bit both sides charged, holding their spears above their shoulders. Stabbing with them, they crashed into each other at a full gallop. Men were down all over the place, and riding animals without riders reared, or trotted in circles, all in a vast cloud of dust. Then the next ranks crashed into the first two, and within seconds, all you could see were men hacking at each other with swords.

Before long the men in the robes were getting overwhelmed, and those who could turned around and tried to get away. The other army chased them, shooting at them now with bows and chopping down anyone they caught up with. There must have been thousands of dead men lying around on the ground, and quite a lot of dead riding animals.

Neither Deneen nor I were saying much when we flew away. But we both were thinking that when it came to savagery, Fanglith had to rank with the wildest of the felid worlds. It was an interesting place to see, but we wouldn't want to live there. One of the things we'd learned in school was that intelligent felids were genetically more warlike and more given to personal violence than humans were. From what we'd seen, it didn't look like it.

The different parts of Fanglith had people of different races that looked more or less like the major branches of humanity in the Federation. And it made sense to suppose that our parents would land in the part where the people looked about like us, an area of probably over a million square miles. That didn't mean that's where mom and dad were, but it made sense to start searching there.

What I actually decided to do was fly a slow grid pattern at fifteen miles above sea level, starting from an ocean on the west. Our detection instrument was Bubba, who lay on the deck beside the control seat, alert to any sign of dad's or mom's minds. We'd been doing this for quite a few hours when he raised his head, his ears forward.

"Here!" he said.

I was surprised it was so soon. Slowing, I made a big circle. "Which way now?" I asked.

He was frowning. "Not sure. Go lower."

I did. "They not together," he said. "Far apart."

"Far apart?" said Deneen. "Where's their cutter?"

"Don't know." He got up and began to pace around, his face with what for him, was a worried expression.

"What's happening with them?" I asked. "What are they thinking about?"

"Can't read thoughts so far. Only close— maybe one, two miles if not many people. Far away, only know they be there."

Deneen had been scanning around while I circled. "Larn," she said, "something flashed down there, something shiny. It's in a forest meadow on the mountainside." While she was saying it, she reached for the magnification controls, and we watched the ground seem to jump up at us. There was the other cutter, sitting among the wildflowers! We were so relieved, we didn't even cheer. We didn't even yip!

Then Bubba threw cold water on our discovery. "They not there," he said. "Not at cutter; not even close. They two different directions from there."

I moved the mass proximity control lever and we started to drop; we were on the ground in less than a minute. That's a nice thing about the distortion drive—no sense of acceleration like there'd be in a floater. If I'd dropped that fast in a floater, it would have squashed us to drop so fast and then stop abruptly the way we did. The last hundred feet to the ground, of course, I took it a lot slower.

And if we hadn't found mom and dad, at least we'd found their cutter. It seemed to me that they were bound to come back to it—unless they'd been arrested by Federation political police or local authorities.

Our equipment locker had two blast pistols, a blast rifle, and two stunners. I got out the rifle and handed it to Deneen, then took one of the stunners.

"I'm going to look the other cutter over," I said to her. "You stand just inside the door here and keep your eyes open. If anyone shows up, other than mom or dad, let me know. And stop them." I turned to Bubba. "And you keep your mind tuned to anyone who might pop up."

"Nobody around here but us," he said. "Not for mile. No danger."

I didn't know what to say to that. I hadn't even thought to ask him! So I just said "good," and went out. But I took the stunner with me anyway.

The other cutter was open, and there was a skinny animal inside, maybe two feet long, including the tail, shiny and near-black. When I came in, it panicked, darted around quick as anything for two or three seconds, then ran down the short aisle and into the bathroom. It was a good place for him; he smelled bad. I looked into each of the little sleeping cabins, then the systems chamber, and finally the bathroom. The animal had left, apparently while I was in the systems chamber, saving himself a headache from the stunner. No one but me was in the cutter. And there was no message, written or in the computer.

So I went back to our own cutter and told them what I'd found. "I have the feeling they haven't been there for a while," I added. "Several days maybe." I turned to Bubba. "Which directions are they from here?"

Bubba motioned with his head. "Dad that way. Mom that way. Pretty far."

"Hoo boy!" I said. "Anybody got any ideas?"

"Sure," Deneen answered. "We fly first in one direction and find out where one of them is, and then the other. Then we decide what to do next."

Not terribly brilliant, I thought, but very doable. I nodded, touched the key that closed the door, then lifted a couple of miles and started southwest. "Is this the right heading for mom?" I asked Bubba.

He nodded.

"How far?"

"Maybe twenty miles."

One thing we knew was that Bubba's expressions of distance got a little vague beyond a mile or so. Twenty could mean anything from about twelve to maybe thirty; twenty was a useful statement of general magnitude. I made a couple of course adjustments on

Bubba's instructions and pretty soon we were parked three miles above a set of stone buildings where he assured us she was. The buildings were connected by high stone walls to form a large enclosed courtyard, and they were 21.6 miles from the other cutter.

Bubba was grinning at me. *One of the worst things in the galaxy*, I thought at him, *is a smug canid*.

His eyes laughed.

The place below didn't look like a fortress, but it was built so it could be defended. Outside the walls were what looked like vegetable gardens. Inside were flower beds, shrubs, and small roundish trees that might be fruit trees. Women in long heavy-looking robes were working in the gardens. The few men we saw there seemed to be guards or soldiers.

When we'd first arrived at Fanglith, I'd instructed the computer to establish a coordinate grid for the planet. That way, any place we might want to return to, we could record on the grid system. Now I entered the information, "mom's location," into the computer for the coordinates we were at.

"Can you pick up anything from here?" Deneen asked Bubba. "Anything about how she'd doing or what she's thinking?"

"No strong feeling now, but she all right," he answered. "About *think*—me not know. Too many minds down there together, and she not think *to* me."

"Can you find dad from here," I asked, "or do we need to go back to the other cutter and take it from there?"

"This way," he said, pointing with his nose.

It was about twenty-five miles, again with a couple of minor course corrections. We took about five minutes to get there, and I recorded the location while we looked the place over. It was a lot like the place where mom was, but bigger, and the fields around it were a lot bigger. Here we didn't see any women at all, only men, and like the women at the other place, they wore robes. There were quite a lot of them working in the fields, hoeing and pulling weeds.

And as with mom, Bubba couldn't sort out dad's thoughts or images from the others.

"Can you tell if he's one of the men working in the fields?" Deneen asked Bubba. "Maybe we could land close by and pick him up."

"No. He inside," Bubba said. "And me think not good for us to be seen. Not go any lower where people are."

"Why?" I asked.

"Not know. Just feel that way."

"Well, at least we know where they are," I said. "And maybe they need to be in those places. Maybe they're doing something they need to do here."

But even while I was saying it, I found myself not believing it.

While we'd been talking, I'd been fiddling with the viewer stick, scanning idly here and there. The buildings were on a slight hill, with a dirt road leading up to the gate. About a mile away, a group of people were walking toward them on foot. Most of the people were more or less ragged.

Then some men came riding out of the nearby forest. They were about as ragged as the people on foot, but the riders had weapons, some of them swords and some bows. I sensed trouble, and all three of us watched. The men with swords jumped off their animals and began to beat up and rob the people. One of the victims held on tightly to a small bag and wouldn't let go, and before we realized what was happening, one of the robbers started hacking him with his short sword. This seemed to excite the other robbers, and within a few seconds several other victims had been stabbed or hacked or shot with an arrow.

When the robbers had everything they wanted, which included their victims' ragged cloaks, they got back on their animals and rode away. The victims who could still walk then trudged on again toward the stone buildings.

The three of us looked at one another. "A nice place," I said.

Deneen nodded. "What do we do now?"

I thought for a second. "I'm going back and lock the other cutter. I'd hate to have people like those bandits get hold of a blast rifle."

Deneen looked thoughtful as we started back. After a couple of minutes she said, "I can't believe mom and dad would leave the cutter like that on their own and leave the door open. Maybe someone was there when they landed, and went over and ambushed them when they came out."

"Well," I said, "the cutter didn't look as if it had been looted. It wasn't messed up or anything." We were directly above it now, looking down at it in the viewer. "And that's a remote place down there. Not the sort of place you'd expect someone to be hanging around."

"True," she said. "And I suppose if people like the robbers we just watched saw a cutter come down out of the sky to land, they'd probably still be running."

I dropped us toward the meadow, then settled the last few yards gently, imagining a band of robbers seeing the cutter land, then running in panic down the mountain, crashing into trees and falling over rocks and blowdowns. "Do you suppose mom and dad have their key cards?" I asked. "It would be terrible if they came back and couldn't get in the cutter."

Instead of answering, she said, "Let me go over there this time."

"How come?"

"It's my turn," she said simply.

I shrugged. It's kind of hard to argue with something like that unless you've got a good reason. So this time I was the one who waited around with the blast rifle, while Deneen walked over with a stunner. I watched her disappear inside. About four or five minutes later she came back out and pressed a key card against the plate, closing the door. Then she stood there with her back to us for about a minute. It looked as if she was writing on the door. Next she walked to the nose of the cutter and knelt down. After that she came back.

"What was all that about?" I asked.

She grinned and held up a marking pen. "It's locked up tight. There was a key card on mom's dressing counter. I hid it outside and wrote on the door where to look for it: directly under the manufacturer's logo on the ship's nose. No one but us on this planet can read it."

"Federation agents can, if they find the cutter," I said.

"No they can't," she answered. "I thought of that." She was still grinning. "Remember that storm last winter when you killed a day of sleet and snow inventing an alphabet for Bubba's language? I wrote it in that—in Bubba's language."

"But can dad and mom read it?" I asked.

"Sure. They'll figure it out. You showed it to all of us and explained it, and we all fooled around writing stuff with it. If I remembered it, they will. Dad never seems to forget anything, and mom left me a note in it once. They'll figure it out."

Her grin went away but her eyes stayed friendly. "You really are a hotshot, brother mine. I'd never have thought of developing an alphabet for Bubba."

"That brings up something else," I said. It was time to change the subject anyway. I've always gotten uncomfortable when anyone praises me. "We need to be able to ask questions on this planet, which means we have to learn the language."

I raised us above the meadow to about eight miles, then slid west about twelve, out over the foothills and valley country where people were. "Why don't you check out the computer and see if Dad got a linguistic analysis program for it. I'm going to look the country over and hope for a bright idea."

I set the viewer on a magnification that

made people on the surface look about the size of large bugs, increasing it now and then for closer looks. The country was more forest than fields by quite a lot. There was a main dirt road that wound through woods and farmlands, climbing eastward into the higher mountains. Smaller roads branched off of it here and there, mostly going to what looked to me like large fortified houses. There was even one made out of stone, like the castles of Grounia. Near each of these was one or more tiny hamlets with two or three dozen buildings—huts and sheds—and a patchwork of fields that apparently were farmed by the people who lived in the hamlet.

But it was the main road that interested me most because it had a variety of people. They walked along in dribs and drabs, most of them ragged and poor. Here and there was someone riding on an animal, or a small group of riders.

Most of the riders were warrior types. They wore armor—the kind that, from a distance, looks like fish scales. I learned later that it's called chain mail. And each of them carried a sword and spear. Some led a pack animal behind them.

Whenever one of the warriors met someone walking, the person or group on foot would get out of the warrior's way, often holding out their hands as if begging. Except for the mounted warriors, most travelers traveled in small groups, I suppose to be harder to rob.

Now and then there was a walker who dressed differently from the others, more or less like the men in the fields where dad was.

They wore gray or brown robes down to their
ankles and a hood that was thrown back in
the pleasant weather. Their heads were bald
on top, and the bald spot seemed to be artificial instead of natural, because usually there
was a ring of hair all the way around it, even
in front.

None of the robed men carried a visible
weapon, although most walked with a staff
about as long as themselves.

"Larn," said Deneen, looking up at me, "the
computer not only has a linguistics program,
but it looks easy to use. All we need to do is
give it a few dozen defined words to start
with, and some sentences. We don't have to
know what the sentences mean. Then it will
tell us what to do next. Apparently it can
develop a whole vocabulary and grammar that
way."

That got my attention, and I started to feel
pretty good. Because now I had something
positive to do, a way to do it, and a use for it
when I got it done.

"Good," I said back to her. "I know just
how we're going to get our words."

FOUR

As I'd expected, when it started to get dark, travelers began to leave the road to spend the night in woods or meadow. I was looking for a language teacher, one whom I hoped wouldn't try to knife me or anything.

I picked one of the robed men who was traveling alone. I suppose he could have been carrying a weapon beneath his robe, but somehow it seemed to me that he, and the other robed men I'd seen, weren't that kind. Beneath a robe didn't seem to be a good place to carry a sword anyway. It would be too slow to get it out.

Really, it looked as if they belonged to some kind of organization, maybe some nonmilitary group. They might even live by nonviolent rules, like the urso-felid mystics of Fylvikh. I hoped.

We watched him walk back into a meadow that had a brook running through it. He walked back a hundred feet or so from the road and sat down next to the brook to eat something that seemed to be bread and cheese.

When he was done eating, he got up on his knees, held his palms together, bowed his head, and just knelt there for quite a while. I had no idea what that was about, unless it was some kind of meditation, like on Fylvikh. After that he did some scratching. Then he pulled up his hood and lay down, shifting around some, probably trying to avoid lumps and stones. A couple of times he sat up and seemed to pick up pebbles that he'd been lying on. Finally, with his head resting on the little sack he carried, he lay quiet.

By then it was dark enough that I switched to infrascope to watch. An infrascope isn't great on detail, but it requires very little light. Before long he was motionless.

I waited until it was totally night. That gave him time to get to sleep, which I figured wouldn't take long if he'd been walking all day. Then we dropped down under cover of darkness, and Deneen let me out about a hundred yards from him, at the back edge of the meadow. When she'd lifted again, I walked along the creek toward him with my stunner in hand. It wasn't terribly dark. Fanglith only had one moon, but it was about half full and gave enough light to see by.

I saw him again at about a hundred feet, and set my stunner on low and broad beam. At fifty feet that shouldn't actually paralyze him, just make his physical reactions a little sluggish. It also ought to put him more deeply asleep. At worst, he might have a little headache for a while when he woke up.

That is, if the Gunner Makloon stories I'd read back home were accurate in things like that.

I aimed and pressed the firing stud.

When I got to him, I hit him on the head with the handle of my belt knife, just hard enough, I hoped, to leave a lump. Even through his hood, hitting him like that was hard to do—a lot harder than zapping him with the stunner beam. When he woke up, he was supposed to connect the bump with the unconsciousness, and explain me to himself as someone who'd chased away an attacker.

If he figured it out differently than that, well, I was a lot bigger, and I had the stunner. I'd just have to be alert.

Meanwhile, he smelled bad. He really needed a bath.

As he was only about ten feet from the brook, I cupped my hands together and dribbled cold water on his face. He groaned and moved a little, and I raised his head with a hand. "Are you all right?" I asked in Evdashian. I didn't have to put worry in my voice; it was there on its own. And it would tell him one, that I was a friend, and two, that I was a foreigner who didn't know the local language. I really was his friend, too, although I'm sure he wouldn't have thought so if he'd known what I'd done to him.

He said something to me, the tone rising at the end as if it were a question. Playing it straight, I said back to him in Evdashian, "A robber attacked you. I chased him away." He wouldn't understand the words, but it ought to sound right to him.

He sat up, took a drinking bag from his sack, and had a drink. Then he pushed his hood back, felt the place where I'd hit him, and said something as if to himself. In Evdashian I asked him how he felt.

He looked at me, clearly recognizing now that I didn't speak his language. I reached out, carefully tapped his head with one finger, and said "head" in Evdashian. He just looked at me. I didn't want him to give me the word for hurt or headache, so I tapped my own and said "head" again.

"Ah!" he said. *"La testo!"*

"La testo!" I repeated. The pickup clipped to my utility belt would be passing on everything that was said to the recorder in my daypack. I reached toward his drinking bag and, after hesitating for a moment, he handed it to me. I'd thought it would be water, but to my surprise, the contents were sour. I decided it must be wine from whatever local fruit they used.

"Wine," I said in Evdashian, and sloshed the liquid in the bag.

"Lou vin," he answered.

"Drink," I said and, without the winebag, pretended to drink.

"Ah-ha!" he said. *"Beure!"* He beamed at me. He realized now that I wanted him to teach me, and he was ready to enjoy it. So holding my left forearm across in front of me, I walked the fingers of my right hand along it. "Walk," I said. From there we did "run" and "jump" and other things like that, and then parts of the body and counting on fingers. "Me" and "you" were easy. His name was Robert, and he was eighteen of the local years old.

Deneen and I had already figured out how old we were in Fanglith years. When you have a ship's astrogational instruments to play with, you might as well have fun with them. We'd computed planetary mass from its measured gravity, and did the same for its moon. Then, from their combined masses and their sun's mass, and their distance from the sun, we'd figured the approximate length of the Fanglith year, assuming a perfectly circular orbit. Next, of course, we'd gotten a simple conversion factor from Fanglith years to Standard years, and vice versa, and figured how old we were in Fanglith years.

Robert was impressed at how young I was, considering my size.

By that time he'd given me quite a lot of words. I probably didn't remember more than a third of them, but they were all on record, and I could use some of them in little sentences, like "I jump," and "you walk."

So I pointed at him and said, "You talk, long." He wasn't sure I meant what I said, so I pointed at him and said it again, and worked my mouth as if I was talking. He shrugged and began to talk, while I nodded to encourage him. After a couple of minutes though, he stopped, probably because I wasn't talking back to him, and because he knew I wasn't understanding it anyway. He wouldn't have understood what the recorder was about, even if I'd shown it to him.

I was pretty eager to find out what the computer would make of all this anyway, so I decided it was time to leave. I took a food bar out of my pocket and handed it to him. "You eat," I said. Then I unwrapped it, figuring the wrapper would be a problem to him. He took a bite, chewed slowly, then nodded and smiled.

"Good," he said slowly in his language. "It tastes very good." I understood the whole sentence, even though "tastes" was a new word for me. It just about had to mean what it meant.

I began to back away, my hand raised as if I were leaving. "Goodbye, Robert," I said in Evdashian.

He raised his hand and waved it a little from side to side. Then he made a sign with it—up and down, then side to side. His face had gone sober. *"Adieu,"* he said. *"Adieu, Larn. Mercie, moun ami."*

I turned away and walked to the road and along it so he wouldn't be left with a big mystery about why I'd leave and start back away from the road toward the forest. I was probably a big enough mystery to him already. I walked along the road until I was out of his sight behind some roadside trees. Then I went back into what seemed to be a pasture because of the animal dung in it. I knew Deneen would be watching with the infrascope. When I stopped, she came down and picked me up.

Within a few minutes the computer did whatever it did to what I'd gotten on the recorder. It came out with a 58-word vocabulary and some of the basics of their grammar.

Some of the words were from the long talk; the computer had figured out approximately what they meant. It also had some possible meanings for some of the others—meanings that had to be confirmed—plus a list of other words it wanted defined. And it gave me a list of questions to ask in the Fanglith tongue to learn the local equivalents of some Evdashian words.

When I went to bed that night, it was with the computer murmuring my first language lesson through the skullcap used with the computer's learning program. Deneen had hers on, too. It works fine for straight memorization.

While I lay there waiting to go to sleep, I realized I was feeling a little sad, and looked it over to see why. It was because of Robert. As briefly as I'd known him, I'd come to think of him as a friend, and I was sure I'd never see him again.

Over the next four evenings we learned a lot more of their language, which was called Provençal. I learned particularly much on the third of those evenings. That was the night I talked with a man called Brother Oliver, who was pretty high-powered mentally.

As soon as Brother Oliver realized I was a foreigner whose Provençal was quite limited, he tried another language on me that he thought I might know. It was called Latin, and quite a lot of people in different countries knew it. But of course I didn't, so we went back to Provençal. There we had at least some common ground.

He was a teacher at heart, and really liked to talk. It didn't matter to him that most of it I didn't understand, though he probably thought I understood more than I did. I'd say something now and then to help keep him going, and of course recording the whole thing. He talked most of the night, and Deneen and I found out most of what it meant only after the computer had worked it over and given us a translation.

Brother Oliver was a good guy, too.

I learned more than Provençal from him. I learned that he and the other robed men I'd been learning from had dedicated their lives to a "religion"—a set of beliefs and practices based on the idea of a being called "God," who was immensely superior to human beings in intelligence and power.

Some of the felid worlds had had religions, too. The religion here not only included belief in a being of supreme power. These people also believed in different levels of beings of intermediate power, between the supreme being and ordinary people. Two of those levels were called angels and saints.

Their particular religion centers on a being of what seems to be next to highest rank, although I'm not really clear on this. Even their system of numbering the years is dated from his birth, and this was their year 1069. His name was Christ, and the religion was named "Christianity" after him. Latin is the special language of Christianity.

It was all very novel to me.

Anyway, after the computer had finished working over the recording, and we'd spent a few hours on the language program again, Deneen and I had what seemed to me like a pretty good basic knowledge of the language. We just needed to expand on it and practice with it. So as far as we could, we talked it aboard ship.

The man I talked to the next night wasn't as interesting or as bright as Brother Oliver, but he filled in some holes in our vocabulary. And I got some very valuable information from him, besides.

Some things Brother Oliver had said made me wonder if the locals might not respond badly to people who flew around in the sky. So I checked it out with Brother Girard the next night. I told him that the day before, just at dusk, a thing like an iron boat had come out of the sky, and a man had gotten out of it. I'd watched from the woods, I said, and after a few minutes the man and his iron boat had gone back into the sky and disappeared.

Brother Girard made a motion in front of himself that I'd learned was "the sign of the cross." This was believed to give the person a certain amount of protection against evil, and you could also use it to help keep other people safe.

"You're lucky he didn't see you," said Girard. "Very lucky. For that was either the Devil or one of his demons. If he had seen you, you would be dead by now, and your soul very likely in Hell."

I asked what would happen if such a thing came down where there were a lot of people— say, at a castle.

"Ah!" he said. "The knights would undoubtedly attack it. That is their duty, and besides, knights are very prone to attack things. If it was the Devil himself, everyone there would surely be killed by him, unless they were marvelously pure in heart." He crossed himself again. "But if it was only a demon, the knights might be able to destroy it."

I'd already concluded that the brothers, and probably a lot of the other people on Fanglith, were likely to exaggerate. Even quite a bit of what Brother Oliver had told me sounded pretty imaginative. But Deneen and I agreed afterward that we'd better keep on being careful not to let people see the cutter.

After Brother Girard, I thought we might be ready to make contact with the monastery and the convent, and get our parents out. But the linguistics analysis program wasn't satisfied. It insisted we needed to talk with someone whose principal orientation wasn't religion. We needed to expand our vocabulary into areas I hadn't gotten into much yet.

My stomach felt a little nervous about that. From what we'd seen and heard, the Brothers of Saint Benedict—monks, they were called—were the least violent people in that part of Fanglith. And apparently the best informed. But if the computer said we needed to contact someone besides the Brothers of Saint Benedict, then I decided I'd better do it.

I'd just have to pick the right person, time, and place, stay alert, and be ready to use my stunner.

FIVE

The next day, from about five miles up, we watched something that was pretty gory but also very interesting. A band of eight robbers— these robbers were on foot—came out of the woods and attacked a group of about twenty unarmed people who were traveling together. It was fear, knives, and walking staffs against swords and savagery. Just as they were getting into it, one of the mounted warriors called "knights" rode over a rise, saw what was happening, and charged, his broadsword raised. Only two of the robbers escaped to the shelter of the woods. He chased down and killed every one of the others.

I knew right then who I wanted to talk to and learn from. He didn't look all that safe to be around, but he was on the right side in the fight, and he was certainly a lot different from the monks.

The problem was how to get him to talk

with me. We'd seen no sign that knights talked with anyone on the road except other knights. And we'd noticed that they didn't usually camp by the road at night. Usually they stopped at one of the castles or monasteries late in the day. Because I didn't have much information about knights, I decided a direct approach was as good as any, so I told Deneen and Bubba what I had in mind.

They didn't raise any objections and, to my surprise, I felt a little disappointed about that. I guess I'd been hoping they'd talk me out of it, and hadn't really realized it. Anyway, like it or not, it was time to get on with it.

I dropped the cutter down into a forested canyon back in the mountains and then flew down the canyon toward the road, skimming just above the treetops. That way, the cutter wouldn't be seen from the road, and hopefully by no one at all. Landing in a small opening in the woods, I got out with my daypack on my back and my stunner on my hip. My clothes weren't like anyone else's around there—I was wearing a jumpsuit, of course—but I could pose as a traveler from faraway India, wherever that was.

Brother Oliver had talked a little about India. It was a faraway country that apparently a lot of people had heard of but just about no one had been to, so it was a good place to fake being from.

Where I landed, the canyon had widened into a sort of rounded draw between low mountain ridges. I knew that about a mile ahead it opened into a farmed valley near a road. I'd go there and meet the knight when he came by. After that I'd have to play it by ear.

By rights I should have kept on feeling nervous, I suppose, but once I was in the woods and walking, I felt cheerful and confident, and decided I might as well enjoy the feeling. Birds were chirping, and the air smelled good, probably from the kind of needle-leafed trees that made up most of the forest.

I hadn't given myself much time to spare. When I stepped out of the cool shady forest into the bright sun, I was about a hundred feet from the road. The knight, riding in my direction, was only about a quarter of a mile away. When I reached the dirt road, I stood on it facing him, wondering what to do next. I was sure he'd never seen anyone dressed like me, or anyone with their hair in a grown-out school cut, for that matter. As he approached, I spread my arms, but he didn't slow down or seem at all interested in going around me. From his scowl, it looked as if he'd ride right over me unless I got out of his way.

So I called to him. Not in Provençal—anyone he met might speak to him in Provençal—but in Evdashian. "Mr. Warrior! I need your help! I really do!"

He didn't stop scowling, but he did stop the massive warhorse he rode on. At a distance of fifteen feet, I could see that he wasn't much older than me. His unshaven beard, thin and downy-looking, was mostly on his chin and above the corners of his mouth, yet his left cheek had a big white scar below the eye that went all the way to his jaw.

He was a little shorter than me, but quite a

bit huskier, even allowing for the chain mail hauberk that he wore. Its sleeves came down only to his elbows, and his hands and wrists were surprisingly thick and powerful looking. All in all, he looked like he'd make a great charging center on our banner team at school, but I doubted that banner would be rough enough for him.

He wore a low conical steel cap with a narrow piece that stuck down along the top of his nose to protect it. The cap fitted over a sort of mail hood that covered his neck and throat. All in all, he looked pretty well protected against the kinds of weapons we'd seen on Fanglith.

His hard blue eyes looked me over: I didn't look like a monk or pilgrim, knight or robber. I had my story ready, though. What I needed now was time to tell enough of it to get his interest.

"I do not know your tongue," he said. "Speak French."

I'd never heard of French, but I supposed it was what he was speaking. It was enough like Provençal that I'd understood what he'd said, and Provençal was the only Fanglith language I knew. I'd have to use it. "Excuse me, sir knight," I said, speaking slowly. "I do not know French. I can speak Provençal though, if not well. I need your help, for I am foreign. I must learn more of this country. Otherwise I fear that, in my ignorance, I will do myself dangerous trouble."

When I'd finished saying it, I felt as if I'd just made the galaxy's weakest case for help.

But instead of just riding on over me, he looked me over carefully.

"Why should I help a foreigner?" he asked. "You are no priest or monk, nor any pilgrim by the look of it. And clearly you are neither knight nor sergeant."

Among Normans in the eleventh century, when a squire completed his training—commonly at age fifteen—he was graduated as a *sergeant*. Knighthood was awarded later, for acts of valor in battle.

I know that now. But at the time I didn't even know what he meant by "sergeant." Apparently though, if I didn't fit in one of those categories, I had to buy help. I wondered if that was part of the culture here, or if this guy was selfish all on his own.

"Uh, I can make it interesting for you," I said. "I—God has given me the power to make small miracles! Miracles that can help fill your stomach along the road." I'd gotten the idea from my talks with the monks that people in Provence, and Christians in general, were really interested in miracles. But the knight's face turned positively sour.

"I am no chaser of miracles," he said. "I've heard many claimed but have yet to see one."

But he didn't move as if to ride on, so I took that as an invitation. And I saw my miracle coming to me: a low-flying hawklike bird swooping along about twenty feet above the grainfield on the other side of the road. I suppose it was looking for some small animal to eat. Almost without thinking, I palmed my stunner from my belt, thumbing it to full power as I pointed it, and pressed the firing stud.

The hawk was far enough away that, even at full power, I wasn't all that sure the stunner would affect it. But instantly it fell out of the air without a flutter.

I turned back to the knight. "I don't know if they're good to eat or ..." I began. Then I stopped, because he looked positively shocked. He turned his head to peer off across the field, and I followed his gaze. For the first time, I noticed several men on horseback about a quarter-mile away at the edge of a woods. Two of them had what might have been hawks sitting on their arms.

"Friend foreigner," the knight said quietly, "pray to God that those folk over there do not connect you with the death of their bird. Otherwise, you are a dead man."

This *was* a dangerous place for someone who didn't know the local customs and taboos! And I suddenly realized that any one of them with a bow could stand back well out of range of my stunner and put an arrow through me! A stunner would be fine against a sword, but I should have brought a blaster, too.

One of the people left the others and galloped his horse through the field, trampling the young crop. Like the knight I was with, this person wore a hauberk and helmet. He didn't carry a bow, and so far he hadn't drawn the sword I could now see at his side. But he glanced toward us as he rode, and I could feel the scowl, even if I couldn't see it from there.

Near the place where the hawk had gone down, he reined back his horse and swung out of the saddle almost like a trick rider. Then he stalked through the foot-tall grain, looking for the bird. It took him less than half a minute to find it. Picking it up, he looked it over and then stroked it. Apparently it wasn't dead.

Then he called to his horse, which came to him at once. With the bird in one arm, and in spite of the heavy hauberk and sword, he swung easily into the saddle and galloped back to his friends. He never glanced at us again.

The young knight looked at me with more interest now. He also looked slightly amused. "That was two miracles," he said. "First you caused the bird to fall. Second, you seem to have gotten away with it." For a minute or two we watched the people with their hawks on the other side of the field. When the rider got there, he handed the hawk to someone else, perhaps its owner. None of them looked across at us. Instead, after about half a minute of examining the bird, they trotted their horses into the woods and out of sight.

"Yes," said the knight, "you've gotten away with it." He looked at me. "What is your name and rank?" he asked.

"My name is Larn," I said. "I have no rank except student, but my father is . . ." I paused, groping for the word. "He is . . . an advisor to rich nobles," I said hopefully.

He didn't look impressed. "Strange that he didn't send you to be trained as a knight, if he is noble," he said. "They must have strange customs in your land."

He nodded slightly then, as if he'd just made a decision. "My name is Arno of Courmeron. I am a Norman." He said it as if a Norman were the best thing on this world to be. Then he moved his horse up beside me and reached down with a hand. "You can ride behind me for a time," he said. "We will talk further."

I took the hand and he pulled. He was so strong it startled me. It was like being launched. I hardly had time to swing my leg over the horse's broad rump before I found myself sitting there holding on to the high back of the saddle. And the hand he'd grabbed mine with was the hardest hand I'd ever imagined, as if the palm were armored. It had to be fifty percent callus.

The monks hadn't smelled as bad up close as he did. I wondered if he'd ever had a bath.

He spoke to the horse and it began to jog along again. I didn't know what a Norman was, but I supposed it meant someone from a certain place. On Fanglith, travel and communication were primitive and incredibly slow. Besides which, of course, they wouldn't have computers to store records and information. In fact, from what Brother Oliver had said, only a few people here could even read and write! Even a lot of the Brothers couldn't— the ones he called "lay brothers," whose job was to work instead of study.

So with such slow travel and communication, and such limited data storage and retrieval, obviously each little part of the planet's land surface had to rule itself. The amount of territory and people that one government could keep track of and defend and rule had to be pretty small. The Brothers had referred to kingdoms and duchies and principalities and imperia and electorates. The computer didn't have all the terms sorted out yet, but they seemed to refer to self-ruling areas of different sizes and importances. Or maybe to how independent they really were. An imperium definitely seemed to be a small-scale equivalent to our word *empire**—a collection of different places and ethnic populations under one ruler. But on Fanglith the places were regions on the planet's surface instead of whole planets and systems.

Anyway, I suspected that a Norman was probably a person from a specific one of those units—a kingdom or duchy or something. I decided I'd better learn more about Normans.

"Excuse my ignorance, Arno of Courmeron," I said, "but I'm such a foreigner that I do not know the word 'Norman.'"

He turned and looked at me, his eyes narrowed. "How do you not know of Normans? All Christendom knows of us. William the Bastard has conquered England. In Italy, the Tancred brothers have conquered most of the south from the Lombards and Byzantines and taken much of Sicily from the Saracens. How did you come here from Italy and not know of us?"

A good question, I thought, but he'd never believe the true answer. I'd just have to feel my way and tell him as much truth as he might be willing to more or less accept. "I've never been in Italy," I said.

"That is the Cenis Pass behind us," he answered. "If you came over it, you've been in Italy." He turned in the saddle as he said it,

---

*Empire here is the translation of the Evdashian word (kuther).

and he definitely looked impatient with what seemed like lies to him.

"Sir Arno," I said, "you may be unbelieving of miracles, but you have already seen one today. The fact is that I did not come here over Cenis Pass on either foot or horseback. Instead of telling you about it, let me show you. Can we get down on the ground for a few minutes?"

He didn't answer right away. We just kept riding. A little way ahead, a broad-crowned tree stood by the road, a tree with leaves instead of needles. When we reached its shade, he stopped the horse. "All right," he said, "show me this new miracle."

I slid off the horse. Arno followed, watching me skeptically. "All right," I said, "first of all I'm a—driven out person."

"An exile," he said. "A refugee."

"An exile," I repeated, "who, with his parents and sister, was driven from his home in a country called Morn Gebleu. We went from there to a country called Evdash."

I watched Arno to see what he thought of all this. I couldn't read his expression, but at least he was still listening. "That was years ago," I went on, "when I was a little boy. Then recently men came to Evdash from Morn Gebleu to take us back there to prison. My parents had to flee for their lives. My sister and I weren't at home then, but we knew that our parents would come to this part of the world if they escaped.

"So Deneen and I—Deneen is my sister— Deneen and I used a miracle to come here. It's a kind of miracle that many people in Evdash and Morn Gebleu use to travel long distances. Let me show you."

I said that last—"Let me show you"—not any too soon, because Arno was starting to look impatient again. Then I walked out into the sunshine and looked up, scanning the blue bowl of sky until I found it, not more than a tiny speck. Arno had followed me, looking skeptical. I pointed upward.

"Up there. Do you see that tiny dark spot?"

He looked up and around, then back at me, scowling again, his eyes narrowed. He hadn't seen it, probably partly because it was just a speck, and partly because he didn't expect anything could be up there except birds or maybe angels.

"Just a minute," I said. I took the communicator from my utility belt. "Deneen," I said in Provençal, "come straight down one mile right away."

Her voice came out of my communicator as clearly as if she'd been standing next to us; she was speaking Provençal, too. "Straight down one mile. Yes, brother dear."

I glanced at Arno before I looked up again. He was too much in command of himself to look really startled at this, but the scowl was gone and his eyes were wider, staring at the communicator. Meanwhile, the speck in the sky was getting bigger, becoming an oblong. I pointed again.

"Up there. You can see it now."

This time he did. "What is it?" he asked.

"A boat made to travel in the sky."

He was looking at me very thoughtfully now, He wasn't scared or awed or even nervous.

"And you can command it by speaking to that amulet?"

"I can't command it from here," I said. "Deneen, my sister, commands it when I'm on the ground. She's the one you heard talking to me. It can only be commanded by someone riding in it. I can say what I want done. Then she does it if she agrees. Ordinarily she agrees."

"And your *sister* commands it."

I nodded. "Right," I said. "When I'm not in command, she is."

Arno was looking at me with something like respect for the first time. At least that's how I thought he was looking at me. "I want to ride in this sky boat," he said.

I kind of panicked then; I knew that something wasn't right. I don't know whether there was a flash of greed in those blue eyes or what. I just knew it wouldn't do to have this muscular warrior on board with his sword and big dagger and hard deadly hands. And instead of being cool and working my way out of it, I snapped, "No! It is not allowed!"

Quick as anything, one of those big hands grabbed for me, and I jumped backward about four feet. My stunner was in my hand before my feet touched the ground. Really! No exaggeration! And a good thing, too, because when his first grab missed, he followed through, lunging after me. He had me by my left sleeve and right arm even as I pressed the firing stud. Instantly he fell to his knees with a surprised look and tipped over on his face.

For an instant I had this terrible thought that I'd killed him. I stared at the stunner in my hand, then saw with relief that at some point or other after shooting the hawk, I'd thumbed the intensity back to low again. I hadn't blown his synapses, just paralyzed him temporarily.

What the stunner does is slow the nervous system way down. It especially affects the extremities—the efferent nerves to the arms and legs. After he woke up, he'd be pretty weak and helpless for a while, especially after being zapped at such close range.

I turned him over, and to my surprise he was conscious, his eyes open. "I forgot about the other amulet," he mumbled slowly and thickly.

He was lying in the middle of the road, and a group of half a dozen travelers were just coming into sight around a woods-bordered curve a quarter-mile away. So I grabbed him under the arms and dragged him off the hoof-beaten surface into the grass beneath the tree. Then I went to his horse and took down the mantle tied in front of the saddle. I put it under Arno's head as a pillow.

"What did you plan to do with the sky boat when you had it?" I asked.

One corner of his mouth twitched in a slight smile, the best he could do just then. "Become the King of Sicily," he mumbled. "Then—who knows? The King of Apulia as well. Perhaps the Emperor of Christendom. A sky boat should be of great value in warfare, especially in winning the support of the barons. And who knows what other marvels might be found on board?"

Even with his nervous system slowed way

down, his intelligent dark-blue eyes were intense. King of Sicily and some other place! Emperor of Christendom! A king, if I understood it right, was a ruler whose power was limited only by the amount of military support he had. And emperors we learned about in history class, back on Evdash.

Those were big ambitions for a common warrior, particularly one who didn't look much older than me. But maybe the obstacles weren't as great on Fanglith, or at least among the Normans, as they'd be back home.

It occurred to me then that Arno was a barbarian, and I had overcome him. He might be lying there thinking about revenge, and waiting for the stun to wear off. Revenge or not, he wanted my "amulets" and my "sky boat." I moved back a few feet and sat leaning against the tree. It might also be a good idea, I decided, to seem like an ally to him while I got as much information and as many new words as possible. Then I'd leave. Staying around him was just too dangerous.

"If you had a sky boat," I pointed out, "you'd also need people who know how to fly it and take care of it."

That's when it struck me that he might be a big help in getting my parents free, in case they were actually prisoners. He could be a lot more than a source of information and vocabulary. Dangerous or not, he knew how things were done here. He was a potential ally for us, if it turned out we needed one.

"And if you ever become a king," I went on, "you'd have a kingdom to run. Worse than that, if you ever got to be emperor, you'd have a whole empire to run! You'd have to, uh, keep the barons under control, settle disputes, collect taxes, and keep track of where the money was and who had how much property. You'd give orders to do things, but then you'd need people to see that they actually got done."

The blue eyes clouded with thought. He knew that what I'd just said was true. It was true with any government; I hadn't lived my whole life hearing my parents talk without learning things. But Arno probably hadn't really looked at it before.

To become the ruler of the Federation or a planet, you needed to be a skilled politician. On a world like this one, you'd also have to be a good general. And then, when you'd made it, when you'd become the ruler, you also needed to be a good executive, and appoint good administrators who could handle situations and routine, and give you good advice. Then you made sure they did. If you didn't see to it yourself that the place ran decently, your rule would be one disaster after another.

On Fanglith, running a country would be pretty tough. Judging by the castles scattered over the countryside, and the walled towns, and the robbers we'd already seen, there wasn't much order and security. Most of the people seemed to be ragged and hungry, while the nobility did whatever they could get away with.

"If we're going to help you get to be king or emperor," I went on, "maybe we can help get you a truly great, uh—I don't know the word. Someone who takes care of things for a king. A chief assistant."

"A prime minister," said Arno.

"A prime minister," I repeated. I'd done it, I decided. I'd gotten him looking at me as someone potentially valuable to him as an ally instead of just a victim. Then my attention went to the half dozen travelers, who were only a couple of hundred feet away now. They'd slowed down, paying a lot of attention to us and talking quietly among themselves. I didn't feel good about their intentions, and I didn't have anything they could recognize as a weapon. To them we were a disabled knight and an unarmed kid.

They stopped at last about twenty-five feet away, and one who seemed to be the leader smiled at me. He was a short, chunky, bald-headed man with thick, stubby-fingered hands and filthy clothes.

"Good day, young sir," he said to me. "What is the matter with your master? Taken ill, maybe?"

Two of the others were sidling toward the warhorse. "Let the horse be!" I snapped at them. "He belongs to Sir Arno!"

They both stopped, looking more cautious than scared. They couldn't see any reason, really, why they couldn't just do whatever they wanted. But they weren't quite sure what to make of me yet. I *sounded* like someone dangerous. The burly leader bobbed his head up and down, and smiled as he took two or three short steps toward us. By that time my stunner was in my hand.

"Well then," he said, "why doesn't Sir Arno tell us to be gone? He seems quite helpless, lying by the road as limp as old rope. And

honest folk needs a living." He sized me up
again, then suddenly pulled a knife and started
for me. I zapped him and he pitched forward,
his mouth falling open. One of the men near
the horse moved as if to climb on, so I zapped
him, too. The others, cackling like kertfowl,
stepped back and formed a little cluster.

"You!" I said, pointing to the biggest, "have
the others drag those two off the road to the
other side!" He got right into being a boss,
snapping orders at his friends, and in seconds
the two I'd stunned had been dragged by the
feet into the grass. The previous leader was
bleeding; he'd fallen on his knife and cut himself. I thumbed the stunner setting up nearly
to medium and put them all to sleep then. I
couldn't keep watching them and I couldn't
trust them. All I could do was hope that none
of them had a bad heart.

But I didn't like it. In a game like this, the
losers were likely to get killed or maimed. I
preferred the kind where you shook hands
afterward and played a rematch in a few
weeks.

"Are they dead?" Arno said slowly behind
me. I turned and saw him half sitting up,
leaning on an elbow. He had to be really strong
to come back that much that soon, from anything I'd ever heard or read about stunners.

"No," I said. "They'll wake up after while.
Then their heads will hurt for a while longer,
but they'll be okay."

"You should have killed them," he said.
"That's what they were going to do to us."

"Are they bandits?" I asked.

"No. Otherwise they wouldn't have held back

the way they did. They are probably pilgrims, going to the Holy Land."

Holy and *Holy Land* I'd come to understand pretty well from the monks, but *pilgrim* I only partly understood. I didn't really understand why pilgrims went to the Holy Land.

"Pilgrims!" Arno repeated. "They'll probably end up slaves or dead men instead of praying at the Holy Sepulcher. I've heard that the Seljuks have taken the Holy Land, and that Christian pilgrims go there at their peril."

He rolled over, got to his hands and knees, then raised himself into a kneeling position. "You're right about the headache," he added.

"Don't get up," I told him. "I don't trust you."

He nodded and gave me a little lopsided grin. "You're a strange one, foreigner. But while you may be ignorant, you are not stupid. You learn."

"That's the reason I came to you," I told him. "To learn. What makes you think you could get enough support to become the king of—what was that place again?"

"Sicily. The granary of the Mediterranean."

I guessed what *granary* meant, but he had to explain Mediterranean to me. Sicily was an island, a big island in the Mediterranean Sea. It produced a very large amount of a food grain called *wheat*, that provided a lot of the bread eaten in the countries around that sea. Apparently bread was the principal food on Fanglith, or one of them.

"Sicily is very rich," he went on, "very fertile, and still held in part by the Saracens— the paynims."

The Saracens, I already knew, were a non-Christian people who had conquered a large part of the world—or at least a large part of the world that the monks knew about.

"Robert the Cunning," Arno went on, "the Duke of Apulia and Calabria, is a Norman. He is also the master of other regions of lower Italy, and most of eastern Sicily, a great captain in battle, and the craftiest lord in all of Christendom, if not the world. But the barons mistrust him, and many hate him, because he undertakes to curb their brigandage. So many rent their swords to whatever rival proclaims himself, whether Norman, Lombard, or even Byzantine—to any but the Saracen.

"With a flying boat I could easily gather to me a few young sergeants and knights at home in Normandy—younger sons free to give fealty where they wish. Using them properly, I could easily make myself master of some Sicilian fief, with a strong castle and its own troop of knights. Then it would be easy to take over some wealthy coastal town. A baron with a flying boat and magic amulets would be the wonder of Christendom, and I could soon enough have an army to do with."

Maybe he could, I thought. Anyone who got to be a king had to start somewhere, unless he inherited the job.

"How old are you, Arno?" I asked him.

"I'll be eighteen before the first frost," he said.

"And you've finished your training?"

"Of course. More than two years ago. If eight years is not enough, one might as well be a villein or a monk."

"And you've already been to war?"

"How do you suppose I won my spurs? Of course I've been to war!"

"I see. I don't know how things are done in this part of the world."

"I was with Roger, the duke's younger brother, when we destroyed the Saracen army outside Misilmeri. We killed or captured every man of them, although at the start they outnumbered us greatly.

"I don't know how many Saracens I killed. Twenty, at least. Our mail is heavier, and our swords. Thus our strokes cleaved them, but theirs most often only bruised, unless they struck our faces or hands." His fingers moved slowly to the big scar on his face. "And our horses are larger, and our formations much tighter, so they could notwithstand our charges nor isolate our men.

"At the end, we were bruised and sore from shoulder to knee, and weary beyond belief, but not many of us had been killed. Until then I'd been a sergeant, with only a few minor skirmishes to my credit. After the battle, I was one of the sergeants chosen by Roger to be knighted for valor."

Another small group of travelers had been approaching on the road, and we stopped talking to watch them, I with my stunner in my hand. They looked at us, then at the six guys lying unconscious in the grass, and hurried by us, looking worried. When they were past, Arno began to talk again.

"When the fighting was over, exhausted though we were, we took the rings and purses from the Saracen dead. And there were thousands dead. The Saracen knights wear rings of great value, and carry coins of gold and silver, to pay their ransom with if they are taken prisoner. But Roger asked a greater ransom for the many who'd surrendered. And when the emir ransomed them, Roger gave to each of us a large purse of gold coins, keeping little of it for himself."

Arno grinned broadly, the first real grin I'd seen on him. "The Saracens have great wealth. It is only right that Christian knights relieve them of some of it."

"Then why did you leave Sicily?" I asked.

"To return to Normandy. And the reason . . ." He sat there for a few seconds as if looking at how to explain it. "Truly, the dream of most Norman knights is not mine," he said at last. "Battles are fine, but they are not enough for me. In time, Robert and Roger will conquer the rest of Sicily, to be sure. And I would doubtless be rewarded with a fief of my own there. But I would never be content to be a baron, for in the lawless south they do little but fight. There is fighting and hardship, and all too often death from one of the fevers that strike armies in the heat of summer there. One fights for his suzerain, and between times he fights brigands and his neighbors, who sometimes are one and the same."

He looked hard at me, as if he wanted me to really understand. "It leads nowhere. While at the same time, there are men in those lands known as 'merchants,' who live in comfort and luxury beyond our dreams in Normandy. Their wealth is unbelievable.

"So I was going home with my purse to buy

a small herd of Norman warhorses. Warhorses of sufficient size are not raised in Italy or Sicily, and are worth a small fortune there. I would drive my horses to Marseille and hire some ship's captain to take us to Salerno or Amalfi. There I could sell them for a fine profit—several times the cost of buying them and taking them there.

"There are risks, of course. One could lose his horses and his life to brigands on the road to Marseille. While on the sea are storms and pirates, and a horse can die of seasickness. But risks are part of becoming a merchant, or of anything worth being."

Now he fixed me with his eyes. "But if we should become partners, you and I," he continued; "we could reach much higher than any merchant or baron. We can rule kingdoms. An empire."

Our conversation had taken longer than it looks like, because I interrupted quite a few times that I haven't shown here, to have him explain words to me. By then a couple of the guys I'd put to sleep had begun to groan, and a pair of knights were in sight about half a mile away, riding westward down the road from the direction of Cenis Pass.

I knew Arno was pretty much recovered, and it felt like the time to leave.

I got up. "Arno," I said, "I'll think about the partnership. How can I recognize you from the sky? The little cloth thing on your lance is too small, even though we can make things look large from the sky boat."

"I'll make a much larger pennon," he said. "A red one, cut from the cloak of yonder pilgrim." He pointed to one of the men in the ditch.

"Good." I began to back away, not willing to turn my back on him so close. I wondered how in the world I could work with anyone I felt that way about. The answer to that was that I wouldn't. I'd let him think I might, but he was just too dangerous to be around.

"And Arno," I said, "one more question. Do monasteries ever hold prisoners?"

He looked at me with a puzzled expression. "I think not," he said, "or rarely. Monks are a peaceful lot. Their purpose is not war, but to see to the proper worship of God and the salvation of souls."

"What about convents?" I asked.

"That's different. I doubt that they actually hold prisoners. But some of the women are there against their wishes, sent by their families because there is no dowry for them or because they refused to marry."

I knew there were other questions I'd wish later on that I'd asked. But just now I didn't know what they were, and so far I'd done pretty well. "And Arno," I said as one of them came to me, "if someone dressed like me walked up to a monastery and didn't know how to speak Provençal or any other language they knew there, what would happen to him? Say he was lost and just walked up and knocked on their door."

He looked at me with a puzzled expression. "I think they would shelter him until they had taught him Provençal, or Swabian, or whatever was the language of the land. Then they would no doubt try to persuade him into their brotherhood." He cocked his head to one side then and raised an eyebrow. "But if he showed them such miracles as you did me, miracles not done in the name of God, they might well think him a wizard, and kill him."

I thanked him and left, jogging up the slope and into the forest, with one eye over my shoulder at first, in case he started after me. Once in the trees, I headed straight for the opening where Deneen had left me. It was in the bottom of the canyon; I couldn't miss it. On the way I called her, and she flew down the canyon just above the treetops, the way I had. She was waiting for me in the opening when I got there.

As soon as I got back on board, I fed the contents of my recorder into the computer, while she swooped back up among the fluffy white clouds that were building over the mountains.

I'd learned a lot in my morning with Arno—a lot more than new words.

SIX

It was definitely time to graduate from the kel Deroop/Rostik Academy of Language and Ethnology. Not that we were all that fluent. And what we had was a mixture of Provençal and Norman French. But I felt as if I could get along with it just fine, and the linguistics program agreed.

Now it was time to get our parents back.

There was no question about it: The place where dad was was one of their male religious communities, a monastery. And mom was in a convent, which was kind of the same thing but for women. These were probably the safest places around unless the people there decided you were a demon or a wizard.

We still didn't have any idea why they were in there or how they got there, which was a weak point in our planning. Deneen agreed with me: It was awfully unlikely that they'd gone there on their own. They wouldn't even

have known there were such places. And neither of us could believe they'd separated from
each other on purpose.

No, whatever had happened to put them
there had been out of their control. They probably didn't even know where each other was,
didn't know the language, and were worrying
a lot, although neither was much for worrying. Dad's style was to make a plan and carry
it out. Mom seemed more likely to wait, see
what happened, and take advantage of the
opportunities.

About two hours before dawn, Deneen put
me down in a field less than a mile from the
monastery. I carried my pack, to look like a
genuine foot traveler. The moon had gone down
and it was really dark, so we'd killed all lights
before landing except for the fluorescent instrument lights on the console. It was chilly
when I got out, and the grass was wet with
dew. Dimly I could make out the monastery,
dark beneath the stars, and started walking
toward it.

My stomach felt nervous and I wished I
could use the cutter's bathroom again. Here I
was, alone in the dark, headed for a big stone-
walled enclosure. Once I was inside, Deneen
would have a hard time rescuing me if I got
in trouble. And in there, in the middle of a
bunch of people, my stunner wouldn't be much
insurance if they rushed me.

Deneen had wanted to have the next piece
of action, and argued that she should get mom
out first. But I talked her out of it on two
counts. One, it was clear that on Fanglith,
women were considered inferior to men. She'd

have a harder time than I would in getting people to do what she wanted, regardless of how smart she was. And two, Arno had indicated that the convent might keep women there who didn't want to be there. Neither of us wanted her getting locked up.

So here I was, walking through the field, getting my feet wet and feeling scared.

Standing at the foot of it, the wall looked higher and more forbidding to me than it had from two miles up. And after I got there, I had to walk quite a way around it before I came to the gate. It had a big metal knocker that I raised and let fall with a hard "clop," three times. In half a minute or so, a little window opened in the door, and dimly I could see a face through it.

"What do you want?" the face asked.

I told him I was a foreigner from faraway Evdash (I'd dropped the India idea entirely), that I wanted a place to rest, and would like to talk with the abbot after he was up. I didn't tell him how far away Evdash was. I didn't want anyone to think I was possessed by a demon. Brother Girard had told me about seeing someone flogged until the demon came out of him. That would be a long flogging if there wasn't any demon to come out and you didn't know how to fake it.

Anyway, the gate watchman disappeared, and nothing happened for about eight or ten minutes. I'd started wondering whether to knock again. It looked like they were going to ignore me. Then the little window opened again, and I had the idea that it was a different person looking out at me this time. There was also a flickering sort of dull reddish light, as if someone were holding a torch.

After a few seconds the door opened, and a stockily built man stepped out with the torch. He looked me over for ten or fifteen seconds, then stepped aside and, gesturing, told me to go in ahead of him.

Inside he took me across a courtyard paved with square stone slabs fitted closely together. Like the wall, the building we went into was made of big stone blocks mortared together, and it occurred to me that they didn't have machinery to build any of this—not power machinery, anyway. People had probably cut out these squared-off blocks of stone with hand tools—cut them just so, to fit. And I supposed that men and animals must have moved them there and stacked them one on top of another to build these straight, tall walls.

Inside the building, I was taken down a short corridor lit by a couple of torches in wall brackets. At its end was a big room about eighty feet long and half as wide. It smelled kind of like the hayloft back home on Evdash, and a little like the way the monks had smelled, and Arno. Like bodies that hadn't been washed since the last time they got caught in the rain or swam a river. The room was lit by what little starlight came in through the windows, and by the torch my guide carried. All I could see were bodies sleeping on little piles of straw on the floor, with their clothes on, or at least their robes.

"Sleep here," my guide told me. "The abbot will no doubt see you after lauds." Then, taking his torch with him, he went back out the door, leaving me in the dark.

"After lauds," he'd said. I didn't have any idea what lauds was or were—maybe another word for sunrise. And somehow I'd gotten the idea that I was very interesting to him. It wasn't anything he'd said; he'd hardly said anything. Probably more than anything it was the way he'd looked me over when he'd opened the gate. I wondered if it had anything to do with my wearing a jumpsuit. Dad had probably arrived in a jumpsuit.

Whatever, I thought. Sleeping was the quickest way to make time pass, and it made more sense than standing there trying to figure stuff out without any data. I walked around in the room, being careful not to step on anyone, until I found an unoccupied place with some straw, back in a corner. I raked it together in my own little heap—a stone floor wasn't my idea of a bed—rolled out my sleeping bag on top of it, lay down and closed my eyes. I wondered if I'd have any trouble falling asleep, particularly with the snoring all around, but it probably didn't take me more than a couple of minutes.

It seemed like I'd only slept a short while before a big bell bonged loudly from somewhere, waking me up. Dawnlight was filtering through dirty windows. My roommates began to get up, yawning and groaning, and I wondered if I was supposed to get up, too. Being still sleepy, I decided to stay where I was until someone in authority told me what to do.

The monks didn't have any beds to make,

and they already had their clothes on from the day before, so in about a minute most of them were out of the room. A couple of them looked at me before they left, as if wondering whether they should get me up. Then they left, too, and I went back to sleep again.

The next thing I knew, one of them was leaning over shaking me. "It's time for breakfast," he said. He stood there watching curiously as I rolled and tied my sleeping bag and stowed it in my pack. Like the monks, I didn't have to dress because I hadn't taken off my clothes, or even the stunner, communicator, and sheath knife from my utility belt. I hadn't wanted to risk losing any of them.

There were about eighty monks sitting in the dining hall when we went in. The tables were made out of planks, and so were the benches. When we reached the serving kettle, I was given a ladleful of some coarse gruel in a wooden bowl, with a slice of some dark, strange-smelling bread, and a chunk of cheese on a square wooden plate. There wasn't any sweetener or juice or milk, or anything like that.

But I wasn't really paying much attention to any of those things just then, because I'd spotted my dad sitting at one of the tables halfway across the room. He hadn't seen me because his back was to me, but he was easy to recognize. In this room of gray robes and shaved skulls, he was still wearing his jumpsuit and all his hair. My eyes were on him all the way to the kettle, and I decided to go over to him as soon as I'd been served.

I wondered if they'd try to stop me. They

didn't. In fact, as soon as I'd been given my food, my guide led me over to sit at the same table as dad, across from him a few places down. By that time I'd realized that no one in the whole room was talking. Apparently the rule was that you didn't talk at mealtimes.

But I didn't need to say anything to get dad's attention. He saw me as soon as I came around the end of the table, and his head jerked up. He looked more than surprised; he looked as if he couldn't believe what he was seeing. I couldn't help grinning, and nodded to him as I sat down. I wanted him to know I spoke the language, so I said quietly to my guide, "Is it all right to talk at the table?"

The man shook his head sharply.

I was hungry and ate fast, even though the food didn't taste very good to me. But dad had a big head start and finished first. He had a guide, too, or in his case, more of a keeper, and as soon as he was done, they got up. I got up, too. My guide put his hand firmly on my arm as if to stop me, and when dad saw it, he shook his head, warning me to sit back down. Then he left. Both his stunner and his blast pistol were on his utility belt.

When my guide and I had finished eating, I was led back out into the corridor. "Where did you find that man?" I asked him. "The one dressed like me."

"You know him?" he asked.

"Yes. I knew him in our homeland. His name is Klentis."

He nodded. " 'Klentis' is all we could understand when he arrived. He is just beginning to learn Provençal, and knows no Latin or French or German, or anything else that anyone here has ever heard before. He was brought to us by Lord Guignard. He is not a Christian, we are sure of that, but neither does he seem to be Saracen or Jew, because he cheerfully eats pork."

"Our homeland is Evdash," I said. "In Evdash they have not yet heard of the Christ. When may I speak to Klentis?"

"Probably later. He works in the shop; he uses tools very skillfully. He carries certain of his own always with him on his belt, though I do not know what they do."

We went outdoors into the courtyard, and he motioned to a bench by the wall of the building. "Wait here and do not wander around," he said. "The latrine is there." He pointed at a low narrow building about twenty feet long, into which a monk was just then hurrying. My nose made it very clear what *latrine* meant.

"I must be able to find you quickly when the abbot is ready to see you," he finished.

Then he left, and I went over and used the latrine. The smell, I told myself, would take some getting used to. Afterward I went back to the stone bench again, to wait as I'd been told. The bench was on the east side of the main building, but the sun wasn't high enough yet to shine over the surrounding wall, so the stones were still chilly from the night. After looking around and seeing no one near, I took the communicator from my belt and held it close to my mouth.

"Deneen," I murmured in Evdashian, "this

is Larn. Talk quietly; I don't want anyone to hear us. Do you receive me? Over."

"I sure do, Larn. Is anything wrong? Have you seen dad yet? Over."

"Everything's okay," I told her. "I just don't want anyone to know I'm talking to someone. Especially someone that no one can see but who talks back. I saw dad a few minutes ago, and he saw me, but we haven't had a chance to talk to each other yet. He looks all right, though. He even has a blast pistol and a stunner on his belt, so he's not a prisoner.

"Now listen. Keep an eye open down here. If you see the two of us together and I wave my arm around over my head, land beside us as quickly as you can and open the door. There's plenty of room to land here in the courtyard, and we'll be in a hurry. But if I don't signal, stay up out of sight.

"The first thing I want to do is find out from dad what's going on here. It may be that he needs to stay here for a while for some reason. You got all that? Over."

She repeated it back to me and we ended off. Then I just sat there looking the place over and thinking that this might not be as hard as I'd been afraid it would be.

I wondered where we'd be in a few hours. It depended on how long it took to get mom back. We might even be outsystem by afternoon, heading for somewhere the political police didn't know about. Some old colony world. Or maybe we'd go back to Evdash, to some community where we weren't known. That was probably the last thing the Federation would expect.

The sun edged up over the wall and shone warmly on me. If the bench hadn't been so hard, I might have laid down on it and slept some more. Then my guide came back out. A couple of other monks were with him—husky, both of them—and suddenly I wasn't feeling optimistic anymore. Somehow I got the distinct feeling that everything wasn't all right after all. But all he said was that the abbot would see me now.

He led me back inside and down a couple of corridors, the two burly monks following close behind. All three of them were tense, not to mention me. We turned a corner and there was dad with two big monks standing by him, too. When we came to them, my guide knocked on a door and announced himself as Brother Justus, with the stranger. A deep voice told us to come in.

We did, all of us. Inside was a room like a study. A grim-faced man wearing a white robe stood behind a table. He was holding a silver cross out in front of him in my direction, as if warding something off with it. A worried-looking monk sat next to him, with a big feather poised in one hand and what looked like paper in front of him. Several other monks stood by.

But I didn't pay much attention to any of them, because there was Arno sitting there, wearing his hauberk, with his right hand on his sword hilt. He was smiling a little, his eyes alert.

"Grab their arms," said Arno, and right away the monks grabbed us. He came over and took both the communicator and the stunner off my belt. Then he took the stunner off dad's, too, along with the blast pistol.

"Why are you doing this?" I asked.

"Quiet, demon!" snapped the abbot. His round face had hard little eyes. "You were in the courtyard, speaking with Satan! One of the brothers heard and saw you through the window above your head, and hurried to me with the news. This good knight was with me, and promised to help."

He sounded very smug and pleased with himself, now that he had us corralled and disarmed. Besides the abbot, three monks stood also holding silver crosses in our direction— one on each side and one behind. I guess they felt that would keep us controlled, but meanwhile other monks still held our arms.

I wasn't an expert on the subject, but I knew that Satan was supposed to be the god of evil, while angels were the assistants of the good god. So I answered, "Sir, I have *never* spoken with Satan! It was an angel I talked with, not Satan."

As soon as I'd said it, the abbot's face went from a look of triumph, to caution. "An angel?" he said. "But you are not even a Christian. You as much as said so yourself to Brother Justus."

"Good sir," I said, hoping this was going to make sense to him, "certain angels are assigned to take care of people who are not yet Christians. Who do you think brought me here from faraway Evdash? And set me on the ground last night outside your wall? It was the angel Deneen."

I glanced at dad, who was expressionless

but watchful, then at Arno, who looked very interested. I think Arno was curious about how I'd talk my way out of this.

The abbot just stood there; he didn't know what to believe. I'd learned from the brothers along the road that Satan was supposed to be a tricky liar, and I suppose that's what the abbot was thinking about: that Satan was a tricky liar and his demons would be, too. But then I remembered something else they'd told me: Satan was supposed to live inside the planet, as if it were hollow, while angels lived out in space somewhere, on a planet called Heaven.

"Look," I said, "let me have my prayer amulet and ask the angel to come down from Heaven for you to see. You know that Satan could not come down from Heaven."

I hoped he knew that; I hoped I had it right.

His face got thoughtful, and I could see he was tempted to try it, but he was afraid. So I made it easier for him. "Or let this knight hold the amulet near my mouth," I added. "He can hold it while I talk to the angel."

He looked at Arno, who nodded. Even so, the abbot stared at me for about ten long seconds more before he spoke again. Finally he said "Do it," and I could feel the monks' grips tighten on my arms.

I didn't call Arno by name. He apparently hadn't told the abbot that he knew me, and it felt right to leave it that way. First I told him to be very careful of the amulet, as it had been given to me by the angel. I knew he wouldn't believe it, but I hoped the abbot would. Then I told him about the operating switch. He would push it to one position to transmit. When I said "over," he was to push it to the opposite position so we could hear the angel's answer. When I said "out," he was to switch it to the intermediate position, which turned it off.

Then I had him hold it in front of my face to transmit. The monks were gripping me so hard that it hurt.

"Deneen, angel of God," I said in Provençal, "this is Larn. Can you come down where the abbot can see your Heavenly boat? I beseech you to answer me. Over."

As soon as I said "over," Arno switched to receive. Deneen didn't answer; the voice that came out of the communicator was a man's. And it wasn't in Provençal at all, or even Evdashian—it was in Federation Standard.

"Klentis kel Deroop, you are under arrest, along with your family and any other traitors you may have with you. Any further radio transmissions must be in Standard so we can understand. I am in a police corvette, standing off the planet with detection gear. Unlike the situation at Evdash, we can assume here that any vessel seeking to depart is yours. If you attempt to escape, we will destroy you without hesitation.

"There are three armed chasers in the atmosphere right now, and we have your position coordinates. So remain where you are, rebel. Do not attempt to run. We will pick you up momentarily."

The abbot's eyes were wide and round. "Surely an angel would speak in Latin," he said, "and that was *not* Latin."

It was Arno who answered him. Obviously the knight was still interested in becoming the King of Sicily and all that, which would require our help, of course, or at least our cutter. "That was Aramaic," he lied, "the language of the Holy Land. I've heard the Byzantine merchants speaking it in the south of Italy, but I understand little more than a score of words in it. Of what was said here, all I caught was, 'Are you being well treated?' "

I tried not to breathe a sigh of relief. I had him push the switch to *transmit* again. I'd send using Standard this time. It was important that the locals *not* understand, while I had to be sure that the Federation people understood fully. I needed them to think that I had the cutter here at the monastery coordinates, so they wouldn't pay attention to people on foot or horseback.

"Deneen," I said, "do not transmit. I repeat: *do not transmit*. I assume you heard the message from the political police just now. Go to the opening where I let you out to question the Norman. I repeat: the opening where I let you out so you could question the Norman. Travel under cover of the trees, and when you get there, sit at the edge of the opening, where you can't be seen from above. We'll drop in and pick you up there. And do not, I repeat, do *not* acknowledge this message. Klentis out."

When I said "out," Arno switched off the communicator.

The idea, of course, had been for *her* to fly to the opening and wait for *us*. We'd get there any way we could. She'd heard the police order; I was sure she'd understand what I meant, even with the way I'd reversed it.

As soon as I'd said "out," I stood there staring hard toward the ceiling for about half a minute, with my mouth half open, as if listening to something none of the others could hear. I even nodded a couple of times. Finally the abbot spoke, looking pale.

"What happened?" he asked. "Why didn't the angel answer?"

I gestured at him as if he were interrupting, and pretended to listen for another ten seconds. Then I looked at him again.

"He did answer," I said, "but not out loud. He prefers to speak directly into my mind, and has prepared me so I can hear him that way. It's much faster. He talked out loud before so you could hear him and know that he's watching over me.

"He wants us to leave here, to go at once to the Holy Land. This knight he commands to travel with us as our escort."

The abbot stared at me without saying anything for a few seconds. He looked sober but still suspicious. "The angel sounded angry," he said.

"Of course he's angry. He's angry because we are being held prisoner. And if you would," I added, "let me have your holy cross. The cross of an abbot will surely help keep us safe along the dangerous road as we go about the business the angel has given us to do."

Brother Girard had told me that a demon could not tolerate the touch of a cross. It would make them shrivel and die.

"Brother Odo," said the abbot, "free his

wrist but hold firmly to his arm and shoulder." The monk holding my right hand shifted his grip to my bicep, and the abbot handed the cross to me, watching intently through narrowed eyes. I raised it to my lips and, tilting my face upward, kissed the cool silver while the abbot stared.

The abbot looked very sober as he decided. "Let them free," he said to the monks. "Let them both free."

"And sir knight," I said to Arno, "return the amulets that the angel gave us."

That took Arno by surprise. It wasn't what he'd had in mind, but he couldn't think of any good way to refuse, under the circumstances. He'd played along with me to the point where he'd look bad if he refused. So he gave us back our things.

"Thank you," I said, and turned to the abbot. "And thank *you* for your hospitality and your Christian help. And for taking care of my friend Klentis while he was here. God bless you!"

Then I didn't say any more. I'd done a good job of bluffing, but as ignorant as I was about things, it would be easy to say the wrong thing and get us back into trouble with these people. We were in enough trouble now with the political police.

But Arno wasn't done yet. "And your reverence," he said, "it isn't necessary that the foreigners have destriers like mine to ride upon. I'm sure that the angel of God will be content if you provide them with good saddle mounts, and some monks' robes against the cold of the mountain passes."

* * *

Arno was an ally all right, at least for the time being. But I was glad our sidearms were on our belts and not on his. Dad and I were standing just inside the stable, watching a monk put saddles and bridles on horses for us. Arno was taking care of his own horse. I guess he figured no one else would do it quite as well as he would. Then a monk shouted in the courtyard, and I stepped to the door to look out.

Somehow I knew what I'd see, and sure enough, passing slowly about a thousand feet overhead was a chaser craft, considerably smaller than a family-model cutter. But she'd be armed with a heavy-caliber rapid-fire blaster in her nose. As soundlessly as it flew, it was only luck that one of the monks had noticed it. Now several were staring up at it, following his pointing arm. It would give them something to talk about here, that was for sure, and if the abbot still had any doubts, this would settle them.

Two minutes later we were on our horses, and the chaser was out of sight somewhere. We were about to test our luck. The stable master told us our horses' names—La Rous and Lou Blonde. Arno's horse was named Hrolf, after the founder of the Norman duchy, I learned later. As we rode out into the countryside and down the dusty road, I started bringing dad up to date on Deneen and Bubba and me.

But not till I told him we'd found out where mom was. I could really see him change when I told him that. He wasn't someone who would worry much about anything. But where mom was concerned, he did worry after all. Mainly, I suppose, because there was nothing he could see to do about it. Now he gave me a kind of one-sided grin, and didn't try to say anything for a couple of minutes; he just reached over and gripped my hand.

When I was done telling him all that had happened to us, he told me what had happened to them. It was pretty wild. Like Deneen and I, they'd flown around looking over the planet for a few days. At one time the rebel group he'd belonged to had talked about establishing a base here. That had been fifteen years earlier. If anyone had ever tried to set one up, though, it wasn't here now—not operational, anyway. And apparently the idea had been leaked to the political police.

Anyway, dad and mom didn't take long to realize that Fanglith wasn't what they'd hoped it might be. But they decided to spend a few hours on the ground before they left, breathing air that hadn't been through the cutter's recycling system a few thousand times, air that smelled like grass and flowers and resinous trees. They'd landed in a mountain meadow just a little below timberline, where there wasn't any sign of people, or anything else that seemed threatening, for miles and miles.

After a few minutes, Cookie, our felid, decided it was safe to go out, and inched down the ramp toward the grass and flowers of the meadow. Once he was there, though, he'd gotten into the spirit of things and began romping around, chasing some kind of jumping insect and generally acting crazy.

Meanwhile, dad had found that there were fish in the little brook flowing through the meadow, and both he and mom went fishing. After a while the sun had gone down, and mom decided she'd better get Cookie back into the cutter before it got dark. But fat or not, Cookie refused to be caught. He'd been shut in too long. So mom followed the silly creature toward the edge of the forest, a couple of hundred feet away, and dad had finally gotten one of the local fish to try an artificial version of an Evdashian silver bug.

That's when he heard mom scream, and he saw that two locals had grabbed her and were dragging her toward the trees. He'd sprinted to the cutter, grabbed his blast pistol, and went charging off toward where they had just reached the edge of the woods. Dad's still pretty athletic, and he was super mad, of course, with his adrenal gland on high. Two more of the locals were waiting with bows in their hands for him to get closer, and he blasted both of them. It must have shocked the others half to death to see them go down with blood and flesh bursting out of their bodies.

But dad didn't get to see their expressions, because just then he caught one of his feet in what must have been the hole of some small animal, and he fell down hard. It not only knocked the wind out of him, but he twisted his knee. He probably wasn't down for more than a few seconds, he told me, but when he got back up to limp toward the forest, he couldn't see anyone except the two dead guys he'd shot.

But he could see tracks—scuff marks in the

dead tree needles on the ground. It was still light enough for that. So he kept going as fast as he could. He was limping pretty badly, but they were having to either drag mom or carry her.

Finally it was too dark to see tracks. But they'd started out by angling along a side ridge that slanted down from the mountain. And when they got to the ridge crest, they'd pretty much followed it. So when he couldn't see their tracks anymore, he just kept going along the crest. He figured they might stop and camp along the way somewhere—that they wouldn't expect him to keep coming in the dark—and if they camped, he might see their fire or smell the smoke.

But he didn't. He just hobbled along until morning, and when daylight finally came, he'd come out into farmland in a valley. He had no idea where the cutter was from there, except that it was way uphill somewhere, miles away, and his knee was swollen and painful. So when he saw some people working in a field, he limped over to them, and one of them took him to the little hamlet where they lived. Someone there apparently went and told the local landlord then, because pretty soon two curious knights came and took him to the castle. The head man quickly realized he didn't speak or understand anything they said, and the next thing dad knew, the two knights had taken him to the monastery and left him.

It was amazing to me that no one had tried to rob him. He was alone, injured, and as far as they could see he was unarmed. I guess there are some people that casual crimes just don't hardly happen to.

We didn't see the chaser anymore that day. As we rode, Arno and I passed the time teaching dad more Provençal and Norman French; he'd gotten a start on Provençal at the monastery. Finally, after several hours of steady riding, we came to the place on the road where I'd met Arno the day before, and we turned off there to enter the forest.

And there came Bubba out of the woods; he'd been watching for us. Of course Deneen had realized what I meant with my weird, inverted instructions. She'd sent him to watch for us, in case we missed the turnoff. Dad and I jumped down from our horses and met him, and he and dad had quite a reunion.

Bubba's a little much for some people when they first meet him. A hundred and twenty pounds of carnivore can seem a little much, especially when it's as hard and physical looking as Bubba. But he didn't faze Arno. It turns out that the Normans are great for big dogs. Hardly ever *that* big, but big. What really got Arno's attention was when we'd talk to Bubba and he'd seem to talk back.

I explained to him about Bubba—how he could talk and also read people's minds. Arno looked pretty sober at that, as if he needed to be careful what he thought about.

But Bubba wasn't paying any attention to Arno. He and dad were too busy horsing around. Then all of a sudden Bubba jumped back and his head went up. He whirled around with a bark of "come on," and took off running hard into the woods. He didn't stop to explain, but the way he said it, we knew he wasn't playing; something serious was happening at the cutter. Dad and I got back in our saddles and started after him.

I wasn't that much of a rider, and neither was dad, but we rode through the woods as fast as we dared. Arno got the idea quickly, and he was a lot better on a horse. In fact, he was super expert. Even with all his knightly gear (he'd dropped his lance), and as big and heavy as Hrolf was, they were out of sight ahead in half a minute, Hrolf dodging through the trees and jumping over fallen timber, Arno ducking under low branches, sticking in the saddle as if he'd been glued there.

Even on horses, though, it took too long to get to the opening. It was uphill all the way, mostly not very steep, but steep enough that before long the horses slowed to a canter and then a trot. When we got there, the cutter was gone. We could see where it had sat in the grass and where the chaser had put down against it. Dad said it had undoubtedly used a field jammer so Deneen couldn't take off, slapped a screamer against the hull to scramble her nervous system, then disrupted the magnetic lock to get in.

I felt pretty awful. Double awful, because we'd not only lost Deneen, we'd lost the cutter, too.

"You've been to the other cutter," dad said to Bubba. "Can you find it again?"

That's impossible, I thought. *We flew there and we flew away, and we've been all over the place since then.* But even while the thought was forming, Bubba answered.

"Bubba not find it," he said, "Bubba just go to it. Not need to find it."

So we started. I'd already been saddle sore when we ran into Bubba. I'd ridden quite a bit when I was twelve and thirteen, but not much at all since then. So the three and a half hours on the road from the monastery had been quite a lot for me. To then spend nine more hours riding cross-country turned into torture.

Part of it was kind of hairy, too, on really steep slopes with no trails, where if the horse fell, you probably wouldn't stop sliding and rolling until you hit a tree or big boulder somewhere. But Bubba seemed to know where it was safe to ride. And if dad didn't moan about a sore rear end, I sure as heck wasn't going to. I might wince a lot, but I wasn't going to complain.

Actually, the mountains were so beautiful that some of the time I forgot how sore I was. They were really something. And now and then we got to rest our poor butts, where it was so steep, or the ground so treacherous, that we got out of the saddle and led our horses. That could be tough, too, grinding up some steep slope until your thighs burned. Arno did it with a hauberk on—it came below his knees and must have weighed twenty pounds or more. To which you could add his broadsword; he'd slung his helmet on the pommel of his saddle. We all sweated when we hiked uphill, but Arno sweated most of all.

If it had been me, I'd probably have taken all that stuff off and just let the horse carry it.

But not Arno. He told me a Norman was no Saracen or Lombard. He'd never let himself be surprised with his armor off.

I was glad dad was there. Whenever I'd look at him, he'd smile at me. It was something that he could smile, after all that had happened.

And now he could make the decisions, which took a lot of pressure off me.

To Bubba, our trek seemed like just a pleasant hike in the woods. He must have walked and trotted twice as far as we rode and walked, scouting on ahead and off to the sides looking for passable routes. And all the while he was grinning, with his tongue lolling out. He was in wolfish glory. Sure we were in deep trouble, and he'd fight or even die for his family, but meanwhile, he'd enjoy what there was to enjoy.

I'll always be a better person for knowing Bubba.

Finally, we angled along a forested ridge where the trees weren't as thick or as big as they had been. We were close to timberline. "Down there," Bubba said when we reached the crest and looked down the other side.

I didn't know how he could be so sure. All I could see were trees, cutting off any view of the canyon below.

"Is anyone down there?" I asked. "We don't want to run into an ambush."

"Not down there," he answered. Then he gestured upward with his head. "And not up there. Not for long way, anyhow."

Because it was steep, and dad and I were rumpsprung, we got off and led our horses down. In the canyon, the sun was behind a ridge, but it was still daylight when we came out into the meadow and saw the cutter ahead—the one mom and dad had come in. When we got there, the first thing I did was pick up and pocket the key card Deneen had hidden in the grass. Then dad moved the cutter tight up against the trees on the south edge of the meadow. It would be in the shade there all day long. Deneen had spotted it from the sun glinting on it; he didn't want Federation agents to do the same thing if we slept late.

After that he fixed a meal—we were suddenly starved—and listened on the cutter's radio for any traffic between the police corvette and the chasers. The radio in the cutter could be tuned to a lot of wave bands, including the various government channels. All we could get on our belt communicators was the citizen's channel.

But he didn't get anything interesting; he hardly got anything at all. I talked with Arno, recording again, mostly about the Normans—how they lived and trained and what they thought about different things. For the warrior class—he called it the *nobility*—fighting was the thing, fighting and conquering, and they trained really hard from little kids on.

And they considered themselves the greatest people in the world. I guess it's not too unusual for a people to think they're the best.

By then it was getting pretty dark, and dad said we might as well get a good night's sleep. Arno slept outside—his choice—and that surprised me. But I didn't question him about it;

I didn't want to risk changing his mind. I'd sleep more peacefully if he were where he couldn't possibly get our weapons.

I'd have thought he'd worry, though, about us taking off and leaving him. Maybe he did it to protect his horse. Bubba had mentioned finding the scent tracks of what smelled like large carnivores, and Arno had said there were two kinds—bears and wolves.

Or maybe he was afraid we might kill him when he went to sleep. Although if we were the kind of people to do that, we could have shot him any old time, outdoors or in.

Dad slept on the deck in the control room where he could hear anything that might come in on the radio. Bubba kept him company. I went to sleep in one of the two sleeping cabins and never woke up once until morning.

SEVEN

It was dad who woke me up. When I got up, I found that my behind and my thighs were pretty sore—sore enough that I walked funny for a while. I was glad we weren't going to ride horses again right away.

I'd been sleeping in my shorts and just got up and went outside that way. I was surprised at how cold it was; I wasn't used to being outside in high mountains. The temperature couldn't have been much above freezing, and the dew was the next thing to frost.

All three horses were grazing peacefully, tethered to picket stakes driven into the ground. I wasn't sure what we'd do with them now. I supposed we'd have to take Hrolf with us; I doubted Arno would give him up.

I went over to where Arno was sleeping, rolled up in a large thick blanket. He must have been sleeping with one eye open because when I approached him, his head jerked up

102

and he rolled out and got right up, quick as anything. I could hardly believe what I saw then: he'd even slept in his hauberk! He'd taken off his helmet and sword, and laid them beside him with his shield, but that was as disarmed as he was willing to get outside a castle's walls, I guess. He'd even kept on his mail collet to protect his neck.

I told him dad was fixing breakfast, then went back aboard the cutter while he went over to check out Hrolf.

They had one of our cutters, and didn't have any reason to think there'd been a second one. And if we were on foot without a cutter, then we didn't have a ship's radio either, so they didn't have to worry about message security on the police channel. So dad had finally overheard some meaningful radio traffic not long after I'd gone to bed, and some more later on. They had Deneen and the other cutter, all right. That was no news. Apparently the chasers were out two at a time now, and what he'd heard were exchanges between them and the corvette. The chasers were to stay out of sight except in capture situations, and to observe all travelers in the district.

Their commander wanted all of us caught, and most especially he wanted dad. But apparently he hadn't come up with any good ideas on how to do it, except to watch for us among the travelers on the ground.

If anyone came up with any ideas, he wanted to know about them. Meanwhile, he said, they'd stay around for "as long as twenty days if necessary." Then they'd leave with whatever prisoners they had, even if it was only

Deneen. There seemed to be a set date that the corvette had to be back at the Federation capital on Morn Gebleu. Dad thought it might be for a show trial of prominent rebels.

I'd never realized that dad had been a *prominent* rebel. I'd always had the idea that he just went to a secret meetings and helped put out an underground newspaper. Of course, he could be considered prominent because his family had been, but it seemed to me that it had to be more than that. He must have been something pretty hot if they still wanted him that much after he'd been gone for twelve years!

As long as they thought we were stranded here without a spacecraft, dad said, they wouldn't get *too* desperate. The worst the captain could expect, if he returned to Morn Gebleu without us, was a reprimand. From the Federation point of view, being stranded on Fanglith was the next best thing to our being dead. The biggest drawback to it was, they were cheated out of giving dad a public trial and execution.

If it wasn't that they had Deneen, we could just hide out here until they'd left. But that wasn't how it was. And whatever we did to get Deneen back, it had to be done in twenty Standard days.

Twenty days Standard was about 23.7 of the local days.

"You know a lot more about this planet than I do," Dad went on. "What do you think we ought to do next?"

"Well," I said, "I don't know how doable this is. But it looks to me as if the only way to them. But when we'd finished eating, dad turned the talk to business.

"All right, Larn," he said, "what do we do next? Explicitly."

I didn't answer right away. I looked at him, and I looked at how I felt about the question. "The next thing I want to do," I told him, "is let you make the decisions. I don't think it should be up to me."

His eyes were steady. "Why is that?" he asked.

Dad likes straight answers to straight questions. And when he looks at you like that—not mean or anything, but with his full attention, and his full *intention*—no putoffs are possible. Besides, you know he isn't going to blow up at you or act like you're a dummy.

"Because you're my dad and I'm just a kid," I told him. "You've got a lot more experience than I have."

He smiled a little, but I could tell he was holding back. He really wanted to laugh, but didn't want me to feel like he was making fun of me. He was remembering times I'd complained that he was treating me like a kid.

"That's true, as a generality," he said. "But on Fanglith, you're the one with the broadest experience. Besides, you've gone along on your own here this far and done an excellent job. It's foolish to replace a winning general, especially when he's been winning against odds."

"But I don't like being the boss," I complained. "Not when things like people getting killed are involved. Besides, Deneen was helping me."

He did laugh then, and I realized why. I

or dad said, I had to interpret. Which isn't all that easy. It's one thing to understand what's being said and another to say it quickly in the other language without losing some of it or changing some meaning.

But actually I did most of the talking anyway. I explained to Arno about the corvette and the three chasers, without saying anything about other planets, of course. Then I told him that dad and I needed help to take control of the corvette and get my sister back—that if he could recruit thirty or forty knights and sergeants, we could probably use them. Their pay would be the corvette—I called it a sky warship—and its chaser craft.

It was hard to know what Arno was thinking, but his eyes sharpened at the part about them getting the warship when we were done. Now he sat there with his lips pursed, looking thoughtful. My eyes went to his right hand—his sword hand—resting relaxed and half open on his lap. It seemed too big for his body size. I could see a thick ridge of callus, hard and cracked, that ran from the end of his forefinger to the knuckle of his thumb. He looked like a hundred and eighty pounds of organic fighting machine.

Anyway, I kept up the sales talk. "The sky warship is much bigger than the cutter," I went on, "maybe bigger than any sea ship you've seen. With it, you could make yourself King of Sicily in a week—king of anywhere in Christendom you want. You could easily drive the Saracens out of the Holy Land. No fortress or army in this part of the world could stand against you, no matter how big it was.

You wouldn't even have to kill very many if you didn't want to."

His eyes locked on mine. "If your people have such mighty ships," he said, "why haven't we heard of them before? With such power as that, why haven't you conquered our land?"

"The world is a lot bigger place than your people imagine," I told him. "A whole lot bigger. There are a lot of countries, and great distances, between my land and yours. My people have heard only the faintest rumors of Christendom, and they have more than enough trouble close to home. Although it would be a good idea for you not to let the warship return to its port after seeing your land."

All this was basically the truth. Here they used "world" to mean this planet and all of creation. Only, the way Brother Oliver had used the word, they seemed to think of them as practically the same thing.

For several seconds he just sat there, thinking. "And how will you get thirty or forty knights to the sky ship?" he asked. "This craft is too small to carry thirty or forty armed knights."

"We can take at least twenty-five in it," I said, "if we stand them in all the available space. Probably thirty. We also need to capture one of the small enemy sky boats that we call "chasers." We'll use dad as the bait, probably, and get one of them to come to us on the ground. It can probably take another three or four knights if we really crowd them in.

"Dad can fly it and I'll fly this one. He'll pretend to be one of the crew and say he captured the cutter. When we get up to the sky ship, they'll open the . . ." I paused. The Normans didn't have any word for hangar. They probably had one for hatch, but I didn't know what it was. "They'll open the side of the sky ship and we'll go right inside. Then we'll get out and capture it."

Just then, saying it, it felt to me as if it might almost be possible.

"How long will it take to fly to the sky ship?" asked Arno, probably thinking about his knights standing in the cutter too jammed together to sit down.

"The time it takes a man to walk a mile," I told him. Brother Oliver had explained the word they used for mile: it was one thousand double steps long—two thousand steps, actually—which made it pretty close to our Standard mile back home.

"And what weapons will we face?" Arno wanted to know.

"If we just went up and attacked them from outside with this cutter, they'd destroy us as easily as this," I said, and snapped my fingers. "It's a warship, and this isn't. The idea is to get inside and take them by surprise. They aren't used to close fighting, and they won't be prepared for it. And they have no idea of the strength and skill and valor of the Norman knight. But surprise is absolutely essential.

"Just a minute," I added, and summarized our conversation for dad and Bubba. "We better show him what a blaster can do," I went on. "He has to know what they could be up against. He already knows what a stunner can do, but we need to shoot up a tree or something for him, with your blast pistol."

Dad nodded and got up, and the rest of us followed him: Arno and Bubba and I. Dad aimed at a tree and pulled the trigger, and an energy charge burst against it with a flash, throwing bark and chunks of wood. Instantly he fired twice more, hitting another tree with one charge and gouging some gravel out of a boulder with the other.

Arno didn't look shocked or horrified the way I thought he might, but he did look pretty thoughtful. Then dad told me some other things Arno needed to know, more encouraging things, and I passed them on, translating.

"It's not as bad as it might look," I said to Arno. "They're not used to being attacked inside their ships, and Dad says their blasters should all be stored in the weapons locker unless they're expecting something like this. They just don't carry them aboard ship.

"We'll meet them at close quarters, and if we surprise them and then take them quickly enough, most of them won't even be carrying a stunner. *If* we surprise them and if we move fast. But they'll have a weapons locker on board, and if we're too slow, then we'll be in deadly trouble, because they'll have time to get out blasters."

He nodded, and unslinging his shield, he held it up in front of him. It was about three feet long and maybe twenty inches wide near the top, narrowing toward the bottom. "Shoot at my shield with your stunner," he said.

That made sense, but I felt a little uncomfortable aiming at it with him holding it. After making sure it was on low, I pressed the firing stud. He was still grinning at me over the shield, so I fired again.

"I can feel a little tingle in my left arm," he said. "That's all."

I could have fired at his lower legs, of course, and he'd have fallen, paralyzed to the hips at least, numb and weak all over. But it seemed doubtful that the political police would think of that in the brief heat of battle.

I borrowed the shield and examined it. It was heavier than I expected, made of some very hard wood that Arno called oak, and covered with layers of what seemed to be thick leather, also very hard. I wasn't sure what would happen if a blaster charge hit it. If it were only a pistol instead of a rifle, it would probably tear up the shield, and maybe the guy's forearm, but the shield still might save his life.

"How many men are there on a corvette, dad?" I asked.

I could see him adding in his head. "Probably thirty-five or so," he said, "including the chaser crews. But they'll be scattered on post in different parts of the ship. If we can take the bridge and the command officers quickly, we should be able to neutralize any further resistance."

Then his eyes fixed on mine. "And that brings up the matter of capturing a chaser," he said. "How do you propose we do that?"

I told him what I'd told Arno. We'd use Klentis kel Deroop to bait a trap. "Only, I'll be Klentis kel Deroop," I said, "instead of you. When they heard my voice speaking

Provençal on the communicator, they thought it was yours. We can just leave it that way, so that I'll be the actual bait. You can be part of the jaws, along with the Normans. If the computer on this cutter has a linguistics program, it'll be easy for you to learn to talk to them."

Then I went on to explain the rest of my plan to him, such as it was. He nodded thoughtfully. It was a long way from being a guaranteed winner, but it was simple. And under the circumstances, it seemed like the best we could do.

First, though, we needed to pick mom up, and that called for approaching the convent at night, which left us with a whole day to do something in. Although it would mean traveling by daylight, I wanted to go and look over Arno's home country and get a feel for it. But dad vetoed that. The chasers would have too much attention on the area we were in for us to travel by daylight. He wasn't even willing to do any unnecessary travel at night.

So we filled up the day doing other things. The computer did have a linguistics program, so I spent a while entering all the Norman French and Provençal I knew, plus the conversation I'd just recorded with Arno. Then we called Arno, who was fooling around with our modern fishing gear at the creek. He came in and talked at length, answering questions about Normandy and the Normans, mostly stuff I hadn't already recorded.

Finally evening arrived, and dad and I went to bed early with the learning programs on.

We'd be getting up a couple of hours before dawn, and the nights were short at that latitude in that season.

The toughest part was getting La Rous and Lou Blonde into the cutter. Hrolf went right in, led by Arno, and we finally got the other two in by leading them up the ramp blindfolded. Then we hobbled all three. Next, using the infrascope and with Bubba guiding, we found the convent again. After that, we found a tiny opening in some forest a few miles away, where we could return to the cutter and hide out.

Then, dad put Arno and me down in a field about a mile from the convent. We took all three horses with us to the convent, the spare being for mom to ride. The sky was starting to get light in the east when Arno rapped on the gate with the hilt of his dagger.

Except that they made us wait until daylight to get in, we had no trouble at all. It helped that I was wearing the robe I'd been given at the monastery, and had the abbot's big silver cross hanging on my chest. They let us see mom, and the way that she and I reacted when we saw each other, there wasn't any question about us being mother and son. So they let her leave with us; it was as easy as that. And when we left, we looked like three locals, because mom was wearing a robe, too.

On the way back to the cutter, she and I filled each other in on what had happened. The bandits had taken her to the main bandit camp, where they'd apparently been heading when they saw the cutter sitting there. After dad had shot two of them with the blaster, they'd been about half scared of her, but they hadn't let go of her even for a minute. She must have looked really strange to them in a jumpsuit, and taller than most of them.

At the main camp, they told their leader all about it. She could tell when they told about the blaster, because one of them imitated the sound and threw himself on the ground with a big flourish. Some of the others began making the sign of the cross then, and the leader knocked one of the kidnapers down and started yelling.

They'd been lucky dad wasn't within hearing.

Then there was an argument for a while. Mom didn't understand the words, of course, but she got the idea from the way they looked at her, that they were arguing over whether to kill her or not. I suppose they figured that dad was a demon, and that she might call him in on them.

Maybe they decided not to risk making him any madder. Anyway, what they ended up doing was taking her down into the valley without even waiting for morning. Then they let her go, and for good measure, threw some rocks at her to drive her away. With enough luck, she might have run into dad when daylight came, but apparently she was in a different area.

From there on, her story wasn't very different from dad's, except, of course, she ended up in a convent instead of a monastery. They'd been kind of horrified there at a woman wearing a jumpsuit, but then they'd gotten her into nun's clothes, and everything was fine.

They'd treated her well enough, and she'd begun to learn Provençal.

She asked me if we'd seen Cookie, and I had to tell her we hadn't. He'd either turned wild and gone off somewhere, or something had killed him. Otherwise, Bubba would have picked him up telepathically.

Bubba met us when we approached the forest, to make sure we found the cutter because we'd never been there, and because things look a lot different when you're on the ground. Arno and I waited while mom got down and hugged him. Bubba didn't have to jump around and act idiotic like some kinds of canids because he could talk. He just licked her face a couple of times, grinned like crazy, and told her how glad we were to have her back.

When we reached the opening where the cutter was, dad saw us and let out the ramp. I motioned Arno to stop, and we let mom go the last few yards alone while we got down and picketed the horses. I figured she and dad might feel a little emotional and not want anyone else there when she went aboard, especially someone like Arno who wasn't a member of the family.

Bubba looked at me, and I could tell he approved of my judgment. I felt pretty good about that. With an espwolf, you don't get approval automatically just because you're one of his humans. You have to deserve it.

Then dad came out on the ramp, grinning, and beckoned to us, and we went inside. He fixed us all something to eat, while he and mom told each other what had happened to them. But when we'd finished eating, dad turned the talk to business.

"All right, Larn," he said, "what do we do next? Explicitly."

I didn't answer right away. I looked at him, and I looked at how I felt about the question. "The next thing I want to do," I told him, "is let you make the decisions. I don't think it should be up to me."

His eyes were steady. "Why is that?" he asked.

Dad likes straight answers to straight questions. And when he looks at you like that—not mean or anything, but with his full attention, and his full *intention*—no putoffs are possible. Besides, you know he isn't going to blow up at you or act like you're a dummy.

"Because you're my dad and I'm just a kid," I told him. "You've got a lot more experience than I have."

He smiled a little, but I could tell he was holding back. He really wanted to laugh, but didn't want me to feel like he was making fun of me. He was remembering times I'd complained that he was treating me like a kid.

"That's true, as a generality," he said. "But on Fanglith, you're the one with the broadest experience. Besides, you've gone along on your own here this far and done an excellent job. It's foolish to replace a winning general, especially when he's been winning against odds."

"But I don't like being the boss," I complained. "Not when things like people getting killed are involved. Besides, Deneen was helping me."

He did laugh then, and I realized why. I

was begging off because, I said, I was too young. Now I'd brought in my fourteen-year-old sister's smarts as part of the reason I'd done well so far. If her judgment had been that helpful, and it had been, then my age wasn't that big a deal.

"Look, Larn," he said, shifting gears, "let's consider this as an internship you'll be doing. You'll be working under the eye of an experienced decisionmaker—me—and I'll step in any time I think I need to. From my experience as a consultant, I'm admittedly better grooved in on making decisions under pressure, but in this case, you've got more and better data. You're also extremely bright. And you've got good sense, which basically means that you seldom enter much mental garbage into your decisions—odds and ends of ideas that don't belong there.

I laughed, a laugh that sort of sneaked up and surprised me. Dad stood there with one eye cocked.

"After the way I've been bobbling around on *this* decision, I'm surprised you haven't changed your mind," I said. "Okay, I'll do it. I guess I was actually enjoying being the boss when you weren't here. Then somehow or other I thought you should be taking care of me again, as if I were a little kid.

"But it would be nice to be playing just for fun, or maybe where the loser has to do pushups."

Then we started talking about details. Arno had told us that Normandy wasn't mountainous, so we could expect to have a harder time finding good hiding places there. Knights spent a lot of time there hunting on horseback, all through the forests and waste places. I certainly didn't want to draw any crowds that might be noticed from above. In fact, I didn't even want the locals to know about us, except selected locals that Arno was trying to recruit.

I asked Dad whether it would be safe to hover a few miles up. It seemed to me that Normandy was far enough from Provence that the political police might not be watching for us up there. We'd just be one small object, stationary except when we were going down or moving back up.

But he didn't feel good about it.

I recalled then that the corvette had said something about having detection gear to spot us and lock in on us with if we tried to leave the planet, and I asked if it could pick us up flying around down here.

"I doubt it," he said, "not near the surface. Gear like that would work by picking up disturbances in the local Q-matrix."

He could see I wasn't understanding him. "I guess," he went on, "I haven't paid enough attention to what they teach and don't teach in high school physics on Evdash. The Q-matrix is actually the energy field which we think of as space/time . . ."

"Oh!" I said. "In school we just called it the space-time matrix."

"Okay. Then you probably know it's disturbed by the operation of a ship's drive."

"I can see how it would be."

"Well, even in mass-proximity phase, a ship in powered motion can be quickly and accurately located at a considerable distance, even close to major nodes in the matrix, like a planet, simply because the drive operates by distorting the matrix."

"But in mass proximity phase, the distortion would be pretty slight," I pointed out.

"True. But not too slight for their instruments to pick up if we're far enough from the surface. Fortunately, in the boundary layer of a solid-crust planet, close to its interface with the atmosphere, the matrix is more or less irregular. Most over mountains and least over an ocean or sea because matric irregularity increases with surface irregularity."

I nodded. I could see where this was leading.

"All right," he went on. "So, close to the surface they can only detect us with other kinds of instruments, like radar and human eyes, that are actively scanning for us. I'm sure that's how they found Deneen—with radar or visually. And because they don't seem to know there's another cutter down here to find, we can hope they won't be scanning for one. We can't depend on that, but when we do have to fly around down here, we can feel a little less threatened.

"Actually, though, I expect their detection gear is just an accessory of their astrogation system. And the astrogation system will be on at all times to maintain the corvette's parking position. So they'll pick up our drive if we get far enough out that we show up as a moving anomaly against the background of matrix irregularity.

"Boundary layer irregularities in the matrix damp out rapidly with distance from the surface. For example, I'm sure that at fifteen or twenty miles elevation we'd be noticed instantly. I'm not sure that even five miles is safe, and I definitely wouldn't go as high as ten. But at two or three miles, I'm pretty sure the danger lies in being spotted by chasers watching the surface."

"And we don't know how big a danger that is," I said.

Dad nodded, pursing his lips thoughtfully. "If they think we're on foot or horseback, presumably wearing local clothing, they must feel that the chance of finding us is close to zero. They may just be going through the motions of a search, hoping, but not expecting much. Which means they might not be watching too sharply.

"But the fact remains that they have three chasers flying around down here, and we can't afford to be careless. So as your consultant and executive officer, I recommend that we stay below three miles at all times, fly mainly at night, and keep our speed under five hundred miles an hour. We'll blend with the natural irregularities better when we travel slowly."

Then, after we'd talked about some other things, mom set up the learning program for their sleeping room while Arno and I went out to talk and nap under the trees. Bubba went outside, too. He lay at the edge of the shade with his nose on his crossed paws and his eyes closed; he'd know and warn us if anyone came near, on the ground or overhead.

We'd get our rest during the day today; tonight we'd be on our way to Normandy. And meanwhile, I thought as I lay there in the sunshine, we had one kind of detection device that the political police didn't. We had an espwolf in the family. Espwolves would never associate with a group like the political police.

I hadn't been asleep very long when Bubba woke me up. As soon as he woofed in my ear, I scrambled to my feet, but he wasn't warning me of anyone coming, only of weather moving in. I became aware of the bumble of thunder not too far off. It wasn't just a thunderstorm approaching, he told me, but a whole line of them. That probably meant a major change of weather. How he knew was beyond me.

For a minute, I thought he was just warning me so I wouldn't get wet, but it was more than that. Sometimes we forget how smart an espwolf can be because Bubba doesn't say a whole lot. Talking is awkward for him. And also, he looks pretty much like an ordinary, if oversized, canid.

So he had to tell me what he had in mind. "Very thick clouds," he said, "very close to ground. We fly near ground or in clouds, enemy no see us with their eyes. And thunderstorms make their instruments no see us, right?"

Who knows what Bubba had learned, eavesdropping on our minds while we did our school homework or read other stuff?

I woke Arno and told him to get the horses ready to load, then opened the cutter and yelled in to dad and mom to get ready to leave—that Bubba said a frontal storm was coming. Then I went and helped Arno. Mom came out to peer up at the sky while Arno and

I brought the horses. All you could see was blue, but outside the cutter she could hear the thunder, too. Bubba explained to her what he had in mind.

It kind of overwhelmed mom to actually see the horses brought on board, crowding the control room. I mean, she could smell that they'd been inside before, but here they were in the flesh! It wasn't much trouble to get them up the ramp this time because we blind-folded them right away.

Then Arno and I went back out and sat on the ramp, listening to the thunder getting closer. Even with the trees crowding around pretty closely, it wasn't more than four or five minutes before we could see the clouds coming in on us, dark bluish-gray and sort of rolling along.

A couple of minutes more and the first drops came spattering down, big and hard and cold. The sky was rumbling and booming now, and we scurried into the cutter and closed her up. Dad had turned on the sound pickup, and we were deafened by a terrific bang of thunder as he took her up and off over the trees.

We were on our way to Normandy, our visibility blurred and limited by driving rain. Arno was our guide: all dad and I knew was that it was somewhere northwest, along the north coast. Pretty soon we came to a river that Arno called the Rhone, and turned north. Not long after that we didn't have a guide anymore, because things looked too different from the air. From the air, Arno didn't have any idea where the road to Normandy left the river. He'd only been through the region once before, and the roads all looked more or less the same—dirt, with wheel ruts, and just wide enough for wagons to go.

The country was at least seventy percent forest, with an irregular patchwork of farm fields. A few minutes up the Rhone, we passed a little town that Arno recognized, called Lyon. Actually it was a big town for this part of Fanglith, and had a large and impressive stone building that Arno called a church. He said the church was God's residence on Fanglith. But when I questioned him, he explained that God didn't live there physically, and that every church was his residence. I decided I didn't have the background to understand that, and dropped the subject.

At Lyon the river forked, and after that we didn't see any town big enough that he could look at it from the air and say, "Oh, that's so-and-so." I took the controls then because from our early scan of the planet, I had a rough sort of idea how the continent lay. Normandy, Arno had said, was on the north coast of France. And if I didn't know where the boundaries of France were, I did know that if I turned and headed west, I'd come to the ocean. Then I could follow the coast northward.

It took us about an hour to reach the ocean—Arno called it the Atlantic—and I kept worrying about coming out into sunlight, where we might be seen from above. We didn't, though. We were under solid cloud cover all the way, with me flying not far beneath the clouds. In places the rain would thin for a little way, and then we'd run into another heavy thunderstorm. The storm was beautiful and the country was beautiful; I wished I could slow down and enjoy it more. A lot of it was even more heavily wooded than it had been along the Rhone.

When we got to the ocean, it was south of us, not west. We'd flown out over a peninsula. Then I did slow down, and followed the coast northwestward until we came to the peninsula's end. From there I followed the coast briefly north and then northeast. Arno watched out the broad, curved, transparent front of the cabin, his eyes intent on the ground, his face expressionless. He hadn't said a thing since he'd admitted he was lost.

"Does anything look familiar yet?" I asked.

He shook his head, and I wondered if he'd even recognize home if he saw it from our angle. There weren't any good landmarks, like a big city or a big mountain. It was forest and more forest, wet and wind-whipped, featureless hills, a sameness of crude castles made of dirt and timber, with tiny soggy hamlets near them and surrounded by farm fields. We never saw one person; the rain had driven everyone under cover. On our left lay gray ocean marked with whitecaps.

Maybe, I thought, we'd have to put Arno down somewhere where he could ride out and ask directions.

After a little while the coast jogged north, then east again, and I stayed with it. There were more farm openings in the forest here, and we crossed a marshy district with drainage ditches and lots of farm fields. We even saw a couple of castles made of stone; we'd only seen one of those all the way across France.

"We're close," said Arno. "These castles are Norman-built." I slowed down some more so he could look things over better. In a few minutes we came to a river with a stone castle near its mouth. "There!" he said. "That river is the Orne! Follow it upstream!"

I did, slowing even more and dropping to about four hundred feet. It was raining furiously just then, the treetops thrashing in the wind, the light more like late evening than midday. Lightning kept stabbing the forest, and we could hear the thunder crash and boom. I slowed way down, as much to watch the storm better as to make it easier for Arno to spot landmarks. He named a castle, a village, another castle as we passed upstream over the valley. Then the valley got narrower and without farms, walled now by timbered hills.

Arno was actually starting to look excited. "There," he said, his finger jabbing, "that road! It goes to my father's castle!"

I turned to follow it. "That road" was a narrow dirt track that left a wooden dock by the river and curled its way through the forest, up into the hills. At that point I was flying about twenty miles an hour. I loved this country in storm, and I was sure I'd love it in sunshine, too. A little dell cut down out of the hills, a creek tumbling and splashing in its bottom, showing itself rainswollen here and there where the trees didn't hide it. Then the road topped out on a sort of low plateau with farms. At one end of a long farm clearing was the palisaded timber castle.

"That's it," said Arno. "The castle of my father."

Right away I reversed direction, backing down the slope a little, and stopped about fifteen feet above the treetops, parking there. "I don't want to be seen," I explained. "Or if we're seen, I want it to be so briefly that they decide they really didn't see anything after all. I want to choose when we make ourselves known, and not start any rumors about the Devil coming. Where should I put you down, Arno?"

"Find a place where the road is wide enough," he said, "and come down between the trees."

I found a place. "Before I put you down," I said, "let's make sure I know what you're going to do here. This first stop is mainly to find out where men may be available, right?"

"Yes. And perhaps to get my brother Charles. Then I'll probably go to see Rufus Shieldbreaker. He has a big family, with many younger sons."

"Younger sons?" I said.

"Yes. Only the oldest son inherits. Younger sons must find their own place in the world. Many went with William the Bastard to help conquer England, but more than a few were returning when I left home. They did not like the restrictions that William was putting on them there; he would hold all the power in his own hands. At the same time, more and more are going to Italy these days, as I did, to join the Tancreds and others there. So it is hard to say from one season to the next exactly where men can be found. But there will be plenty."

"Where and when should I pick you up?" I asked.

"In the open on top of the hill, beside the road, in the hour before dawn. Travelers are few up here at any time, and at that hour, none."

"Make it earlier," I said, "so we can take you wherever you need to go next and be hidden again by daylight."

"In the second hour then," he said.

I landed. It was good to get the horses out. I had him take all three of them. He could leave ours with his father and get them back if we ever wanted them. The cutter was a smelly mess; it wasn't designed as a horse stable.

Arno rode off with his cloak over his armor and his hood up. The storm had slacked off for the moment, but it was still raining, and water was dripping from the trees. I kind of wished I was going with him, but I didn't trust him. He could easily decide to settle for our little cutter and take me hostage for it, instead of going for the corvette. Or some baron with his squad of knights might make the decision for him—just sort of take the project over and crowd Arno out. From our talks, I'd gotten the idea that Normans in general could be treacherous as well as rough. Arno had certainly shown that he could be, when he tried to take my stunner away from me that first day.

I didn't understand yet how much the Normans loved to fight, though, or how reckless they could be, or really, that big ambitions were not unusual among them. Most of the Norman nobility preferred playing for big stakes, even with big risks, rather than for little stakes with small risks. They'd definitely prefer a corvette to a cutter.

EIGHT

After Arno had left, I lifted again, almost to the cloud cover this time. Then we flew around over the countryside looking for places to hide, places that would be all right when the weather cleared, and where we'd have the best chance to go undetected by the locals. I recorded the coordinates of a few possibilities, but none of them really seemed very good. While this part of Normandy was considerably more forest than field, there was always a castle and an area of farmland not too far away from any hiding place, and the natural openings mostly looked more or less marshy.

Besides that, one of us on the ground would have a hard time finding any given one of the hiding places if he needed to go to it; there just weren't any good landmarks. Not including Bubba, of course; he wouldn't have any trouble at all.

Afterward, we still had most of the afternoon left, and I felt restless. It seemed like there ought to be something valuable for me to do that would take advantage of the stormy weather. Mom went into their sleeping room and settled down with the learning program, while dad sat beside me and watched out the window.

So I flew back down the River Orne to the coast. Along the ocean there were cliffs behind the beach, and I found one hiding place that looked pretty secure. There was a cliffy little ravine that cut back into the tableland and came out about three-fourths of the way down the beach cliff. The tableland above the cliff was forested, and there were clumps of trees in places in the bottom of the ravine, so there were lots of places in it that couldn't be seen from the air. An Evdashian orek would have a hard time climbing in there from above, and from below it would be impossible without mountain-climbing equipment. The brook that ran down it was tiny, even in this weather, leaving plenty of room to park on dry rock. We could hide in there for months.

Of course, we didn't have months, and hiding wasn't what we'd come to Normandy for. But I felt a little better knowing about it, just the same.

Then, just for the heck of it, I flew on northeastward up the coast a way, to see what was there. Basically, it was more of the same.

Meanwhile, something was still bothering me. I decided it was the waiting. I didn't really know whether twenty days was plenty of time, or too little, but it seemed as if we ought to be doing more—that we ought to be *hurrying*.

On toward evening, we landed in the driest-looking opening I'd found in the neighborhood of Arno's father's fief, Courmeron. The rain had about stopped, but the sky was still dark and cloudy, with occasional drizzles and showers. Dad suggested that I get some sleep if I wanted to, and I did. I can almost always go to sleep if I want to, just by lying down and closing my eyes, and it's better than biting my nails.

Over the next three days, Arno went to three different castles. We took him to the first one and he rode to the other two. He didn't have much to say when we saw him, but he seemed to feel good about his progress. He was sizing things up, he said, and being mysterious to get people interested.

I didn't feel good about it, though. He hadn't shown us one recruit yet, and time was passing.

Meanwhile, we heard a little radio traffic between chasers and between the corvette and the chasers, and they sounded pretty bored. Our instruments showed us that the chasers, when they'd talked, were still down south in Provence. So we stopped worrying so much about being seen by them, although we still didn't take chances. Hopefully, though, if they came north, we'd hear about it in advance.

Also, even after the storm moved out, the weather mostly stayed showery, so we didn't worry much about local hunters running into us. And, of course, when Bubba was around, we had his special security talents.

But some of the time he wasn't around. He spent a lot of time at night exploring the countryside.

Another thing with Bubba—this was his idea—he tried the learning program and it worked about as well for him as it does for humans. So he learned the Provençal/Norman French hybrid, now more and more Norman French, that we had in the computer. Knowing the language is helpful to a telepath because people often think verbally, even when they aren't talking.

To pass the time, we humans started practicing "hand-foot art"—a system of unarmed fighting that was illegal now in the Federation. It had evolved on some planet or other, during the old imperial days, for self defense against personal assaults by imperial troops. Systems more or less like it had developed on several planets, actually. Later they spread around some.

It became a tradition in some families, including dad's, and when the Glondis faction took over the government and outlawed the practice, the main result was that it was practiced secretly instead of openly. Dad taught mom and, later, Deneen and me. We were rusty now because we hadn't done it for a while—not since we'd left Evdash—but I got right back into it again. My parents had to work back into it more gradually; dad was fifty and mom was forty-one.

I wished Deneen were there to spar with. She was the most skilled in our family—the quickest and most flexible, and as precise in execution as dad was. I'd never used it in an actual fight; we were forbidden to except to save our lives. On Evdash, they didn't even know that hand-foot art existed, and it would have marked us as off-worlders for sure.

So the closest thing we'd ever had to real fights, with real contact, had been with a padded robot that dad designed and built. His name was Lurt. Lurt was programmed to do various moves in scrambled, unpredictable sequences, depending partly on what you did to him. Lurt could be set for various levels of quickness, but he couldn't hit too hard. And you couldn't damage him at all.

Before dawn on the fourth morning, Arno was waiting at the meeting place when we arrived. The previous days we'd been there first. And this time he wasn't alone: he had three sergeants and a knight with him. He wanted them to see us, and more especially to see the cutter come in and land, so they'd know it was real and that he wasn't crazy.

They all wore hauberks and helmets like Arno, and swords, and they all looked tough and dangerous. But I sort of got the idea that Arno could take any of them in a fight. One of them, Brislieu, was quite a bit bigger than the others and looked enormously strong. But Arno had a kind of air about him that made me think he was the most dangerous—surely the smartest and most controlled. When we shook hands, each of them had a grip a lot stronger than mine, and I was considered strong back home. And like Arno's, their right hands were heavily callused. I supposed this came from lots and lots of practicing with heavy swords all their lives.

There wasn't a lot to say to them. They were there mainly to know that we were real, and Arno had already told them as much as he wanted them to know. After we'd talked for a few minutes, dad and I went back into the cutter and lifted to about twenty feet as a demonstration. Then they started off for another castle, and we went to our next meadow hiding place. We weren't to meet Arno for two more days, and time was shrinking, but at least his progress was visible now.

Bubba did some recruiting, too. The next day he didn't come back from his night's excursion until on toward midday. I'd just been wondering about him when I glanced out the window and saw him sitting about fifty feet away, staring at the cutter as if mentally commanding someone inside to open up.

And just back of him, at the edge of the trees, were four of the local wolves! They weren't as big as Bubba, though one of them came close to it. They were gray, compared to his russet brown, and their heads weren't as massive, either in actual size or in proportion to their bodies. But overall, they looked a lot like him.

He saw me looking and came over to the cutter, next to where the ramp would be when I sent it down. I did, and went out on it.

"Hello, Larn," he said. He didn't wait for any questions. "I want you meet four friends of mine, and they meet you."

I got the feeling that this meeting was important to Bubba, and also that it was delicate business. I could guess why. The wolves here had had bad experiences with men. Arno had said as much once when I'd explained that Bubba's species had been wild until recent times. That's when Arno had taught me the Norman word for wolf—*leu*—and distinguished it from *chien*, their domesticated canid.

So I got down on my knees and hugged Bubba. Then we started to tussle and he knocked me over and we rolled around for a minute, rassling. We'd rassled lots of times before, but this time it had a special purpose. We were demonstrating our trust and closeness, and that neither of us was subservient to the other.

My parents had heard Bubba's voice but not what he'd said, and looked out the door. "Don't eat the captain," mom said to him. "Or I'll be terribly upset." She stepped out on the ramp with dad, and Bubba and I separated and I got up.

"Klentis, Aven," Bubba said, "I want you meet four my new friends."

The local wolves were still sitting at the edge of the trees, taking this all in. Dad raised both hands overhead with his open palms toward them, as if to show he wasn't holding any weapon. "Welcome," he said to them. The word wouldn't mean anything to them, but presumably they'd get the idea.

"Are they telepathic?" I asked Bubba.

"Yes. That how they accepted me leader. I not even have to fight. They read me, know me smartest."

"Their leader?" mom said. "You're not, um, leaving us for a new pack, are you?"

He grinned. "While we in this place, I stay with them most of time. They interesting, they good people, and they maybe help us. But you people my pack; we have more in common. When you leave planet, I go with you."

"Good," I said. "You had me worried for a minute. What did you mean, they maybe help us?"

"They maybe help you catch enemy chaser."

"Really?"

"They not foolish—not waste their lives. Not like some canids. But if pretty good chance help you, and I lead them, they do it. Probably."

"But you're not sure," I said.

Bubba did what he does instead of shrugging—he twitched the hide on his shoulders. I don't know whether it's an actual espwolf thing or something he thought of on his own to help communicate with humans.

"They say they would—they believe it in their minds. But if things so dangerous they not in control of selves . . ." He shrugged again. "They very good people. Pretty smart, too. Not reason so good as you and me, but more than most animals. And they have *honor*."

It occurred to me that I'd never heard him say "honor" before. He's always had it, and so have we, but it just hadn't come up in conversation. I wondered how he'd score on a human intelligence test. Or how I'd score on an espwolf intelligence test! Deneen swore that he was the most rational member of our family, and from her, that really meant something.

Meanwhile, there he stood grinning at me! The rascal knew everything I'd been thinking.

Then he glanced back at the local wolves, and apparently thought something to them because one by one they stood up and walked toward us in a row, the biggest one in front. Dad and mom came down the ramp to meet them. All four circulated among us, sniffing us. We did our getting acquainted with our eyes, looking them over, noticing the ways they differed from each other.

"Bubba," Mom said, "the way the human mind works, we like to have names for people. It helps us sort them out when we think and talk about them. Will they mind if we name them?"

He stood for a few seconds as if listening, then shook his head. Mom looked at the biggest.

I'll name you 'Biggest,' " she said, "because you are." Then she looked at the others, one at a time. "And you are 'Blondie' because you're so light-colored. And you are 'Slim' " —Slim was rangy and long-legged—"and you are 'Wise Eyes.' "

"Are those names all right with you?' she finished.

They looked at her steadily without moving. "They heard you," Bubba told her, "and it all right. The idea of names strange to them, but they content with it."

"What about the rest of the pack?" dad asked. That took me by surprise; I'd assumed these were all of them. Then I realized that only one of these, Wise Eyes, was a female. It made sense that there'd be more than one female.

"They in den place, with little ones. We go

back to them now; you stay here." The five big canids turned then and trotted toward the nearby trees. Partway there, Bubba paused and turned to look back at us.

"These people fear and hate humans of this planet," he said, "who always try hunt them down and kill them. But they know intentions, good, bad. They say again they help if they can."

Then the wolves disappeared into the forest, leaving us staring after them, and wondering what Bubba had said that made them willing to help.

They also left me thinking. It would be tough to be a less intelligent large animal sharing a habitat with primitive man and competing with him. By the time he felt secure enough and civilized enough not to try to wipe you out, you could easily be extinct.

NINE

The second night after he'd ridden away with his four recruits, Arno told us he wanted me to come with him. He wanted to show me to some new prospects he'd lined up to join us, and he wanted me to give a demonstration of our weapons. Also, he wanted dad to fly over the castle low enough to give them a good look at the cutter. In daylight. Then he'd tell them that the warship was much bigger, with much more powerful weapons.

"Why by day?" I asked. "If he hovered at fifty or sixty feet at night, they could still get a good look at him."

"By night," he said, "some might think the Devil had sent it. The Devil prefers the darkness." He grinned. His grin could take you by surprise because he usually didn't show how he felt. "You're lucky you fell in with Normans," he went on. "If we were Franks or Lombards or Britons or Saxons—maybe even Swabians—

we'd *know* you were from the Devil. But Normans are willing to look and take a chance."

His grin widened. "Besides, the Devil is not a fool. He leaves Normans alone. There are those who would say we're bad enough without him. If he bothered us, we'd flay and quarter him and feed the pieces to the hogs."

If that was supposed to be funny, it didn't make me laugh. I hoped they didn't decide I was the Devil.

The castle he wanted to take me to belonged to a baron named Roland, who was interested in the project. Roland had just inherited his fief from his father, who'd been killed fighting river pirates on the Orne. Now that Roland was the baron, with knights and sergeants of his own, he was looking for adventure. Specifically, adventure that would make him richer and more powerful.

Arno was sure he could bring Roland in on our project, once the baron saw a blaster in action and a cutter in flight. And Roland would automatically bring in with him five knights and five sergeants that were his personal men—landless knights with money fiefs. Add these to Arno's own men—they were up to six now—and Arno said he could easily get the rest of the thirty or forty.

I felt uncomfortable about visiting a castle. All we needed was to have Deneen a prisoner of the Federation and me a hostage in a Norman castle. But I couldn't very well refuse to cooperate with Arno in recruiting because we depended on him for troops, and the days were slipping by.

Dad must have realized what was going on with me. "Larn," he said, "I have a suggestion."

"Go ahead," I said. I could use all the help I could get.

He looked at Arno and then at me. "If you go, I'd like to arrange a demonstration against the castle gate. At noon today." He turned to Arno again. "Even this little boat has power you haven't seen yet, and it's not built or intended for fighting. It has none of the attack weapons you'll have when you've captured the warship. But even so, I can destroy the castle gate with it. And that should not only impress this Roland, it should make him think twice about treachery toward us."

I had no idea how dad intended to destroy a castle gate. The biggest weapon I knew of on board was his blast rifle. It had quite a bit more power than a blast pistol, but there was no way it could take out a castle gate, or probably even make a hole in it. But dad wouldn't have said what he'd said if he didn't have a plan he felt confident about.

Meanwhile, Arno was looking at dad, but what he was seeing was inside his own Norman mind, I was willing to bet. I could almost see it, too—a mental picture of himself in a big fancy hall, wearing rich robes and being crowned Emperor of Christendom, with thousands of knights cheering and holding their swords overhead.

So I agreed to go with Arno. We would set up the people at the castle—the baron and his knights—to expect to see a sky boat around midday. Arno said that if they were expecting it, and if they already knew it was simply a magic boat with people running it instead of demons, they wouldn't jump to any weird conclusions about the Devil being in on the deal. Especially, he said, since they'd have seen me by then. He said anyone would know that I wasn't a demon.

Arno also said that the priest who lived at the castle and took care of its religious services was no fool. His loyalty was to the baron as well as to God, and if the baron went for the project, the priest wouldn't object to it unless I wore horns and breathed fire.

The fly-over would be a signal to Arno and the baron. When the call came that the cutter was flying over, we'd all go out where we could watch, and see what would happen.

Arno had brought a horse for me, and before long I was riding beside him through the darkness. I don't know what there is about it, but on Fanglith or out camping on Evdash, it seems as if the quiestest part of the whole night is the hour before it first starts to get light. I could hear hardly a sound except the soft thudding of our horses' hoofs on the dirt road, and some distant animals, probably small, that made a sort of "greep greep" noise. The "greep greep" sound reminded me of pond hoppers on Evdash. Off to the northwest I could see a bank of clouds that might mean more rain, but most of the sky was clear, and the moon was high in the east, about half full.

After about a mile, we rode past a farm hamlet where a canid began to bark, and then two more canids. About that time I could see the castle in the darkness, not far ahead. I'd seen it before, from overhead, but hadn't paid much attention to it. It hadn't seemed important to me then.

As we got close to it, I began to make out some details. Its outer wall was the usual palisade of logs set in the ground, probably deeply. Outside the palisade was a big ditch, fairly deep, with shallow, stagnant-smelling water in it. The palisade itself turned out to be about fifteen feet high. There were a lot of the greep greep sounds coming from the ditch. A bridge crossed it, to the gate, and when we clopped our horses out onto it, the nearer greep greep noises stopped.

Two armed men were waiting and let us through the gate, and we helped them close it after us. Inside the palisade was a good-sized area that I would have called a courtyard but the Normans call a bailey. It was mostly open, but had some buildings in it that seemed to be barns and sheds made of squared logs. They were mostly backed up against the palisade.

The main building, the manor house, was in the middle, on top of a steep mound, surrounded by another palisade. It was a square building with a small wing, and looked more impressive than most manor houses I'd seen, partly because it stood on the mound, but also because it had two tiers of narrow windows indicating two stories plus the loft. The shape of the mound was so uniform that I was pretty sure it was man-made, too. They'd probably used the dirt from the ditch to make it with.

When we'd climbed the steps to the house, there was a man, a servant with a torch, waiting, who let us in. Arno took the torch from him, and we went on by ourselves, up a narrow inside stairway to the second floor and along a hall to a room.

It turned out that knights in this castle lived more comfortably than the monks where dad had been. Here they'd put Arno in a room by himself, with a real bed which I would now share with him, smell and all. It even had a mattress filled with some soft stuff.

I'd never seen Arno take off his hauberk before. He wore a kind of knee-length dress beneath it, made of what seemed to be soft leather. I suppose it was to keep the chain-mail hauberk from rubbing the skin raw.

I lay there for several minutes thinking that I might not be able to go to sleep. Everything was too strange, and I'd already slept about six hours. But the next thing I knew, Arno was telling me to get up. When I opened my eyes it was daylight, and I was scratching.

Arno, with his armor back on, took me downstairs to have breakfast in the "great hall." It was damp and smelly, and several big rangy dogs lay around as if waiting to be fed. For some reason, the floor was strewn with long coarse grass.

Around a long table sat the baron and his ten warriors, plus Arno's six, and a man who was dressed like a monk. I guessed right away that he must be the priest Arno had mentioned. Counting Arno and the baron, that made eighteen knights and sergeants—an awful lot of deadly warriors in one room. They ranged from short and stocky, about five feet

two, to Brislieu at about six feet two. But they
all looked hard and strong, and reckless, as if
they wouldn't hesitate to do anything.

The youngest two probably weren't more
than about fifteen years old, but they seemed
to be considered as much men as any of the
others. The oldest might have been forty or as
much as fifty. It was hard to judge, because
he had no teeth, or no front teeth anyway,
and might have looked older than he really
was. He looked as if he'd kill anyone the baron
told him to, without even blinking.

Arno introduced me to them, and we sat
down while servants brought in our food. I
could hardly believe how dirty the servants
were. The only thing dirtier than their clothes
were their hands. I was glad I'd taken a broad-
spectrum anti-infectant when Deneen and I
arrived at Fanglith.

The food included a mush that seemed to
be made of some kind of ground seeds. They
put something they called honey on it—a kind
of sweetener—that was pretty good. There was
also roast meat, hard bread, cheese, and a
stew of vegetables. Basically, it wasn't bad,
except that it seemed to be poorly prepared.
Honey was the best of all.

People ate with their fingers and their dag-
gers, so I pitched in and did the same thing.
Not having a dagger, I used my belt knife. We
washed the food down with beer, about the
same on Fanglith as the beer on Evdash except that it was warm and kind of sour, and it
seemed to be weak, as well. Dad made his a
lot better.

When we first went in and Arno had introduced me, the men had looked me over openly. The baron's men didn't look as if they thought much of me, I suppose because I didn't wear armor or carry a sword. And maybe because I didn't look like someone who could knock down a horse with his fist.

The priest, though, looked at me very suspiciously, his lips thinned and his eyes narrowed. I realized right away that I needed to be especially careful with what I said in front of him. He'd never chop me down with a sword, I was pretty sure, but if he decided I was a demon, I was really in trouble. He'd seen the abbot's cross hanging from my neck, I'd noticed that, but he didn't seem as impressed by it as I might have hoped.

Then we'd all gotten busy eating, and nobody said much. When we were pretty much finished, the baron looked at Arno.

"So this is one of the sky men," he said. "What can he do?"

"He'll show you," Arno replied. "Call in a serving man."

The baron looked at him as if he were trying to figure out what in the world he had in mind. "Otis!" Roland bellowed, and a fat, red-faced servant came hurrying in.

Arno turned to me. "Sir Larn," he said, "be so kind as to demonstate your amulet on this villein."

Be so kind! I looked at poor Otis. He wouldn't think I was so kind. He'd never done anything to me and probably never would, but I was supposed to do something to him. Mentally, I asked him to forgive me; at least this wasn't going to be fatal or actually damaging.

Getting up from the table, I said, "Otis, go back five paces and get down on your knees." I figured the demonstration would be more effective if he was farther away from me.

I could feel the baron's eyes on me, puzzled. Otis backed off and got down on his knees, looking worried, as I turned to the baron. "I don't want him to injure himself when he falls," I said.

Then I pulled the stunner off my belt, turned the intensity control to intermediate, and zapped poor Otis. He fell right over. Everybody but Arno and I stared at him.

"Is he dead?" the baron asked.

I was afraid things might get ticklish if I said the wrong things here. The baron had to be satisfied without offending the priest. I'd just have to remember all I'd learned from Arno and the monks and do the best I could. I decided that the simplest way to handle the situation was to relax and wing it.

"No," I answered, "he's not dead. He could be, though. I can kill a man, or put him to sleep, or just paralyze him. Otis will wake up after a while with a headache. I see no point in killing an honest servant and a Christian."

He looked at me for several seconds, his thick black eyebrows bunched up in a frown. "Come with me," he said, getting up. "Come with me, all of you." We trooped after him out into the bailey and to the stable, where the stablekeeper met us at the door.

"Bring out Man Stomper!" the baron ordered.

The stablekeeper was probably an old knight. Instead of kind of cringing, like the servants

I'd seen, he stood straight, wore a dagger on his belt, and had a look of self-respect. He paused for just a second, then nodded.

"Yes, my lord," he said, and went limping off to one of the stalls. I wondered what Man Stomper would be like. What the stablekeeper led out to us didn't look ferocious. It wasn't even a warhorse. If I had to guess, I'd say he was probably a hunting horse.

"Stand back, Rainulf," said the baron, and the stablekeeper backed away from the horse. Then the baron turned to me. "Do to the horse what you did to Otis," he said.

I didn't know if the stunner would knock out something that big or not, so when I drew it, I turned it to *high*, and adjusted the beam to narrow. Then I pointed it at Man Stomper's head at a distance of about fifteen feet, and pressed the firing stud. He went down as if someone had hit him with a giant hammer. Rainulf stared at him amazed, then knelt and turned back one of the horse's eyelids. After that he felt its throat as if looking for a pulse.

"The beast is dead," he said. He sounded impressed and not too happy.

The baron pursed his lips, then nodded. "No one has ever been able to ride him anyway," he said. "It serves him right for being so difficult." Then he turned abruptly and led us back into the manor, where we sat down at the table again.

No one said anything right away, but I could almost hear the wheels turning. Arno looked like the felid that got into the cream. The baron passed the beer pitcher around the table and everyone but me had some. I felt bad,

about the horse especially. I wouldn't mind
zapping some political police, but I didn't feel
at all good about Otis and Man Stomper.

For the first time since they brought Otis to
me, I looked at the priest, just for a moment.
He didn't look quite as suspicious as he had.
And the hostility that I'd felt from him, along
with the suspicion, didn't come through as
strongly.

The baron took a long swig of his warm
beer, wiped his mouth on the back of his hand,
and belched loudly. Then, turning to the priest,
he said, "Father Drogo, show the sky lord the
castle. Let him witness the lads in training,
and whatever else he'd like to see." He laughed.
"See if he can recite his catechism, if you'd
like."

He glanced around at the others. "The rest
of you find something to do. I will talk with
Arno privately."

They nodded, all of them looking pretty serious. Whatever scorn they'd felt for me before I'd zapped poor Otis had disappeared,
and killing Man Stomper had established for
certain that I was someone to respect. Which
told me what these guys considered important. But I reminded myself that they were
the only kind of people here who could possibly help us recover Deneen.

I left with Drogo and got the grand tour.
First he showed me where the unmarried
knights and sergeants lived—a single room
with wooden beds and shapeless mattresses
like the one I'd shared with Arno the night
before. I'd begun to wonder if the mattress
was the source of the itching that was trou-

bling me. Maybe some kind of insect. I'd noticed the others scratch occasionally at their legs while sitting around the table, and I wondered what they did about itches under their hauberks.

Some villeins had already dragged Man Stomper away when we got to the stable. Rainulf didn't seem to like me very much, so we didn't stay there long. After visiting the smithy, which was also where weapons were made, we went to watch the kids training to be knights. There were five pages and six squires training at the time. The drills and exercises they were doing told me something about how the knights got so hard and strong-looking. I'll bet they weren't any harder on Federation marine recruits in training than the Normans were on these kids, and a couple of them couldn't have been more than seven or eight years old!

Even the littlest ones wore armor, and carried shields and practice swords. They ran with them, rolled, tumbled, and went through fighting drills, swinging, thrusting, jumping, parrying, ducking, and dodging. They also sparred with one another, beating on each other's shields and at any exposed body part. Their drill instructor shouted occasional directions or chewed them out, or stopped them to demonstrate or make corrections. He was scarred and gray, with a noticeable limp, probably a veteran of many battles.

The scars on Arno's face and hands, that I'd supposed he'd gotten in battle, he could easily have come by on the drill ground of some castle before he was ten years old.

We also watched a couple of the younger squires work on their horsemanship. The things they had to do, I wouldn't have believed if I hadn't seen. They were practicing running toward their horses from the side and springing into the high-backed saddles with a sword in one hand and a shield on the other arm, wearing their calf-length hauberks. They must have just about killed themselves when they were first learning.

Finally Drogo took me to the chapel, which was a small wing on the manor house. The floor seemed to be of thick boards or maybe split logs, without grasses spread on it. Benches were lined up for sitting on, probably enough for all the nobility at the castle, including the families of the married warriors. I doubt, though, that it would accommodate the servants at the same time. At one end was a little stand about chest high to Drogo, with a big cross carved on it, and near it a table. Otherwise, there wasn't much there.

"Your name again?" the priest asked.

"Larn," I said. "Larn kel Deroop. The kel Deroops are an old and noble family in the land I came from."

"Um." He examined me again with his narrow eyes. "Do nobles not wear armor in your country?"

"No. My people are mostly peaceful. There is little need for armor. I have never seen men in armor there."

He didn't say anything right away. "Then why . . . that?" he asked, at last, pointing to the stunner on my belt.

"As in any land," I said, "certain men are

evil. It is sometimes necessary to protect one's self, although I had never carried one of these until I came to this land and saw how violent men are here."

He nodded thoughtfully, and it seemed to me then that I was winning his tentative approval.

"And what gods do you worship in your land?"

My relief of a moment before evaporated. I realized that this was the number one question. If I answered this one wrong, I'd blow it all, at least as far as Drogo was concerned. He knew the difference between simply wearing the cross and being a fellow Christian. And Arno might easily have been overoptimistic about Drogo going along with whatever Roland liked. His enmity or disapproval still might decide Roland against us; I could even end up dead here.

"Father," I said, "in my land, the poor unfortunates believe in no god at all. Once upon a time they believed in false gods. But then they learned that they were false, and abandoned them, and never learned about the true God. I have learned a little about him, from some good monks, and about his son, the Christ." I looked down at the cross on my chest and raised it with a hand. "It was the abbot of Saint Steven at Isere who gave me this to keep me safe on my quest."

The way he looked at me still wasn't hostile, but I could see that he wasn't satisfied yet that I was okay. "What are you here for?" he asked me.

"To rescue my sister," I told him.

"I have heard about that. It is not what I meant. What brought you here before they captured your sister?"

I told him the story I'd told Arno about being refugees separated from our parents, and that we'd come hunting for them. "And while I found our parents, who were being sheltered by the children of God, I lost my sister."

He didn't answer right away, just looked at me with his intent eyes. I tried not to squirm. Finally, he said, "And what will you do if you get your sister back?"

The hairs on the back of my neck crawled. *Careful*, I told myself. There was more to this question than just curiosity, and it felt as if his eyes could see right through me. "We will hunt for a land less warlike and dangerous than this one. If we do not find such a place, perhaps we will return to Normandy or Provence."

His eyes weren't on mine any longer. They were aimed off across the chapel, but they didn't seem to be looking at anything there. After a few seconds he nodded slowly. Then, without saying anything, he led me to the door. It felt as if he wasn't really satisfied, but didn't know what else to ask. As he reached for the door handle, it was pushed open from outside, and a little boy came in, apparently a page on errand duty.

He stared at me for a moment. It wasn't as if he was awed or impressed by this strange foreigner, although I'll bet he'd heard all kinds of rumors. He just looked curious—curious and alert. "Father," he said, "his lordship wants you to bring the sky man to his apartment, right away." Then he turned and ran off down the corridor.

Roland and Arno were waiting for us, and Roland got right to the point. He wanted to see dad's demonstration and he wanted to see me use my blast pistol.

For dad's demonstration, he'd have to wait till noon. But I provided him with an immediate demonstration of the blast pistol, and I sure as heck didn't disappoint him. In fact, I made about the best impression I could have. As quick as he asked it, I grabbed and drew my pistol like someone in a holodrama, and blew apart the pitcher on the table—blew it to slivers. Without pausing, I next blew a hole in his door and then set fire to a big fur that was hanging on the wall.

The whole thing took three seconds; then I stood there like Dirty Dirk Degbar in *The Marauders of Melfan*. The baron stared at me for three seconds, then ran over and pulled the fur off the wall. He put out the fire in it by wiping it around in the water that had been in the pitcher.

Arno was looking at me with a little smile. After that, he asked me to leave while he had another private talk with the baron. I didn't go back to Father Drogo; he might have more questions for me. Instead, I went out to the drill ground—not the one in the bailey, but outside the outer palisade, where Drogo had mentioned that the men worked out. There I watched the knights and sergeants training, some on foot and some on horseback. I don't see how any of them survive to middle age.

It was just before the noon meal when dad flew over the castle at about two hundred feet, blowing his warning siren. I turned at once and trotted back in through the gate. He started to circle, and a minute later the knights and sergeants galloped across the bridge, while the gate guards closed the gates behind them. Meanwhile, the whole place came outdoors and into the bailey to stare up at the circling cutter, including the women, little children, and servants. And, or course, Father Drogo was there. Everyone was standing well back near the gate in the inner palisade.

I told Roland to have his people keep well away from the outer gate. Roland, puzzled, gave the order. From his expression, I realized that Arno hadn't told him just what the demonstration was going to be. Then I walked out away from the crowd and waved my arms to get the attention of the cutter. It gave a sort of little bob of recognition, and I clapped a fist into the other palm overhead.

The cutter made a big turn out away from the castle, and I couldn't see just what happened next, except that, at the end of the turn, it was flying slowly back in toward us, toward the gate. Then the palisade cut it off from view. After a few seconds it floated in over the bailey with the door open in the cutter's side.

So far nothing had happened. It swung back around the way it had come, making a half circle outside. It was higher now, though, and I could see dad at the door, which meant that mom was flying it. He pointed his blast rifle, and an instant later there was a big explosion at the gate. The gate burst inward, broken, to hang at an angle from one of its hinges.

It took a lot more than rifle fire to do something like that. The only thing I could think of was that dad had some explosives on board and had made a bomb. He'd come in slow and close, and tossed it out to roll against the gate, or close to it. Finally, he'd detonated it by shooting into it.

It was more evidence suggesting that dad, back in the Federation, had been more of a revolutionary than he'd ever told us kids about. I'd always thought of revolutionaries—the kind of revolutionaries that used bombs—as angry and violent people, at least a little bit crazy. Dad had always seemed mild and rational. His kind of revolution would be a revolution of ideas. But I guess he could be selectively violent if the situation called for it.

By the time our ears had stopped ringing, the cutter had flown out of sight. The servants who had run outdoors were on their knees, making the sign of the cross in front of them. Some of the knights were crossing themselves, too, but not on their knees. The baron was staring with his mouth clamped shut and his forehead creased.

I looked at Father Drogo. He looked thunderstruck.

Then we went back inside to talk some more. I took it for granted that Roland would now agree to join us.

TEN

We went back to the dining hall, where Roland called for more beer. But when the page went to pour some for me, I told him I wasn't allowed to drink more than one a day—that this limit was a custom among nobility in my country. The fact was, I wasn't used to drinking—at home dad would pour us kids a mug only on festive days. And although the local beer seemed to be weak, I didn't want to risk getting fuzzy-headed.

Roland scowled; I guess he felt I'd offended his hospitality. Arno didn't even blink; maybe he knew my real reason. Father Drogo's eyes were back on me again, and I had no idea what he was thinking.

"Well," Arno said, looking at Roland, "you have seen what one small boat can do, with a crew of one man, one woman, and a dog. It is easy to imagine what we can accomplish with a warship. A kingdom can be ours, and then an empire."

"Um-m."

Apparently Roland wanted to dicker about something.

"You disagree?" asked Arno.

"As you say, it is easy to imagine," Roland replied, "but something else to bring about. I have not seen this warship and neither have you. And if it is so powerful, how are we to capture it?"

Arno was starting to look irritated. "I have already explained that to you."

Roland nodded, trying to look wise and reasonable. "True. But ... the odds against success sound damnably poor."

Just then the baron sounded ... treacherous felt like the right word. What he said was true all right, but the way he said it ... He was up to something—maybe even he didn't know what just yet. I got the feeling that he was sort of feeling around mentally for some way to trick us.

He stood up. "Nonetheless, I admit the project has its attractions. Let me confer with my priest on the matter."

The more he said, the worse it felt. Roland didn't even sound like the same man I'd listened to that morning—rough and ready. Now he sounded oily, phony, and that could only mean he was up to something.

He and Father Drogo both left the room, along with the oldest of Roland's knights. I looked at Arno. He didn't look a bit happy. He knew Roland better than I did, and looked like he distrusted him now at least as much.

The baron and the priest were gone for about five minutes, and when they came back, the older knight wasn't with them. Now Arno really looked grim. Father Drogo didn't look happy, either. He didn't look hostile or distrustful, just plain unhappy. I felt almost sure that Roland had ordered the priest to do something bad—something he didn't want to do.

Roland came to the table but didn't sit down. He leaned his big fists on it and looked sternly at me. That felt phony, too. "It is up to Father Drogo," he said. "He will question you further. If he decides you are not from the Devil, then I will agree to take part in this venture, if Arno and I can agree on certain points. But if Father Drogo decides against you, then you must leave, and consider yourself lucky to go with your life.

"Meanwhile, I must talk further with this knight"—he indicated Arno—"about leadership, and who receives what, should I decide to join with you."

I looked at Arno. He and his six men were my best insurance, and now I was supposed to leave their protection. If Roland had people waiting to take me hostage, I could try to fight my way out with my blaster, and might succeed in spite of the bows and arrows I'd seen around. But it seemed to me that that could kill the whole project for us, and we'd never rescue Deneen then—not in the time we had left. So I couldn't just start shooting; I needed to stick with it and see what I could manage.

Arno gave a little nod. I swallowed the lump in my throat, got up, and left the room with

Father Drogo. I only flinched a little bit when I stepped through the door. No one was waiting to grab me, not there anyway, and we went down the hall toward the chapel, Drogo leading. When we got there he opened the door and motioned me through. But his eyes were trying to tell me something, and he gave a little warning shake of his head as he started to speak.

"Enter, Sir Larn," he said. "We have much to talk about."

"Of course, Father Drogo." And with that I darted forward, crouched low, giving the door a sudden hard push backward with my shoulder as I lunged through. At the same time I was drawing my stunner, and at the end of my lunge, I whirled. Behind the door was the older knight. One of the sergeants stood waiting with his back against the wall on the other side. In their hands, both had stout clubs of firewood, which they dropped as I thumbed the firing stud on the stunner. Unfortunately, Father Drogo stood explosed in the open door as the stunner beam swept from one warrior to the other, and he went down, too.

Well, I thought, that would give him a good excuse not to start yelling an alarm. And this way, nobody would accuse him of treachery against the baron. Now I had to get out of there as quickly as possible without alarming anyone.

I grabbed Father Drogo and pulled him into the chapel, then closed the door. Then I checked my stunner. I was sure I'd set it back to medium after shooting the Man Stomper, and sure enough I had. Medium was still pretty heavy duty, of course, but Father Drogo was the oldest and least strong, and his pulse was still beating evenly, so I figured I hadn't killed anyone.

There was a table in the chapel, with different kinds of metal dishes and things on it, well-shined, and a table cloth that went all the way to the floor. I grabbed the old knight by the feet and dragged him there, then rolled him under it. He was heavier than I would have thought, and probably all muscle. I did the same with the sergeant. Father Drogo I didn't drag by the feet; I took him under the arms and pulled him. He'd done what he could for me, and I owed him the extra courtesy.

With them out of sight, I straightened up and looked around. Somehow I felt strong and sure of myself just then, really about as good as I'd ever felt in my life. Seeing nothing more that needed doing there, I went out a back door of the chapel. It definitely wouldn't do to go back into the hallway, where I might run into someone from the meeting.

I didn't go around to the steps that led down the front of the mound, either. I just trotted right down the grassy side and out an unattended back gate of the inner palisade. Then I headed for the stable, checking the sky as I went, on the off hope that dad was still up there with the cutter. He wasn't.

Rainulf was in the stable, filing a horse's hoof. (Horses' hooves aren't split like a gorm's; they're a single piece.) I told him to bridle and saddle my horse for me. He didn't ask any questions, just nodded and did it while I waited there in the smell of horses, hay, and

horse wastes. It's not a bad smell at all, in a
barn. Not like in a cutter. When he was done,
I led the horse out, looking back when I'd
gone through the door, to see if Rainulf looked
at all suspicious. I was prepared to put him to
sleep, too, but he was already back filing the
hoof again.

I climbed into the saddle, jogged easily
across the sun-soaked bailey and out the gate,
saluting the gate guard as I passed. He sa-
luted back. Once over the bridge, I kicked the
horse into a trot and headed down the road,
westward, the way I'd come.

I reviewed my problems as I rode. They
might come after me or they might not. Roland had seen the blaster in action, but on the
other hand, he was a Norman. And from what
I'd seen and heard, Norman meant reckless. If
they hunted me down and didn't do anything
too foolish, they could probably kill me. He
probably felt he'd blown the deal anyway,
and was no doubt ready to settle for my blaster
and stunner, and my dead body.

What Arno might do under the circumstances, I had no idea. He might even go along
with Roland on the hunt, on the basis that if
he couldn't have a warship, he might as well
settle for the blaster or stunner, too.

The next question was, when would they
start after me? If Roland expected word back
immediately from the knight or from Drogo,
he'd start wondering pretty quickly, and send
someone to the chapel to see what was going
on. They might already be searching for Father Drogo and the knight. Or he might just
assume for a while that everything had gone

as he'd intended, and still be talking with Arno.

I looked back and saw nothing except the castle, half a mile back now, and kicked the horse into a canter. My next problem was where to go. From the air, I knew where dad would have the cutter, but I was also pretty sure I couldn't find it from the ground. It was a small wet opening maybe eighty feet across, in a big stretch of forest. I could probably get in the right general area, but find the meadow? I could pass within a hundred feet of it and never know it was there. And I didn't have time to go quartering through the forest in a real search.

Also, the worst place to have Roland catch up with me was in woods. They'd have the trees for cover, they'd be able to surround me, and that would be that.

And I couldn't hang around near the predawn meeting place. It was too near the castle. They could use their dogs, and have me before the afternoon was half over.

Another problem was that the Normans all seemed to be expert horsemen. I wasn't. Off the road, especially in the woods, I couldn't go nearly as fast as they could. Oh, my horse was fast enough all right, and these Norman horses were easy to manage. A little pressure with the reins on one side or a nudge with the heel in one flank, was all it took to steer them. Arno had taught me that. The problem was to not fall off while running full speed in the woods or on rough ground.

But on the road I had at least one speed advantage: Although I was taller than all but two or three of them, I probably weighed less than most of the warriors. and I wasn't wearing a heavy hauberk, or carrying heavy weapons.

Meanwhile, I was headed west. That was the direction of the River Orne. I wouldn't worry about finding the cutter and my parents. I'd let them find me, with Bubba's help. The main thing I needed to do was lose any pursuers, and the river would help me do that. Then I'd hide out somewhere or other.

In another half mile the fields ended, and the road entered the forest. So far, I hadn't seen any sign of pursuit, and I was starting to feel pretty confident. When my family picked me up, we'd fly over the castle with the loud-hailer on and tell Roland he could have us either as his friend or his enemy; the choice was his. Maybe we'd have his help to rescue Deneen yet.

Actually, he'd been no more treacherous than Arno had been, I reminded myself, when Arno had tried to take my "amulets" that morning in Provence not too many days ago. Yet our deal with Arno had been working out all right.

But Arno didn't feel to me like a criminal, the way Roland did. Arno was just being a Norman, and I'd liked him almost from the beginning. I didn't totally trust him, but I liked him.

The road went through forest for most of a mile then, and the terrain was kind of hilly. After that it was more level, and there were farm fields on both sides of the road again for about half a mile. I passed a small castle with an unditched palisade, off to one side, but no one galloped out to challenge me. So far, I'd had the road all to myself.

I'd slowed my horse to a trot again because I didn't have a good feel for how long he could canter without wearing himself out. I didn't want to find myself with an exhausted horse under me if I suddenly needed speed in an emergency. Trotting, though, seemed effortless for him, as if he could do it all day.

Also, a trot wasn't conspicuous. If I kept him at a canter, someone might wonder what I was hurrying for.

When we got into forest again, though, I speeded him up for a while to get a bigger lead. When, if, Roland started after me, he'd probably push his horses as hard as they'd go, probably with hunting hounds leading the way.

When I thought of hounds again, my optimism shrank.

Along the road, a lot of the land was cleared for farming. Then, a few miles and three castles farther, the road began to wind its way downhill through rough, wooded country. It seemed to me that they had to be after me by now, and I let the horse speed up on the downhill. My behind was getting sore again, but I couldn't afford to get off and walk.

The hilly country leading down to the river— the riverbreaks, we'd call it on Evdash—was heavily timbered. Some of the trees were big enough that two people together couldn't have reached around them. Leafy branches formed a roof above the road, letting only spots and patches of sunshine through. The light there had a softness, and it seemed to me a tinge of green as well.

Lush green Normandy was a beautiful place. I wished the situation were different, and that I could slow down and enjoy the country more. Meanwhile, I kept pushing, and after a while came down to the river.

This was the part of the Orne that didn't have a wide gentle valley. Wooded hills came down almost to the water. Another narrow dirt road ran along this side of the river, not far from its banks. There was also a crude wharf here on the riverbank, but no boat, which was fine with me. I knew just what I wanted to do and, guiding my horse around the end of the wharf, rode out into the water. He didn't mind a bit, and the water felt only somewhat cool on my legs.

I started angling downstream toward the far bank. What I had in mind was to take to the woods there for a little way, headed north toward the sea coast. It might not be very good riding through the woods—I couldn't see any road over there—but I'd be out of sight to anyone following the road on the east side.

The river was about two hundred feet wide, and didn't take long to cross. And the woods on the other side weren't very brushy except right along the bank, where more sunlight reached the ground. So it wasn't hard going for the horse, and we trotted right along. Now I could enjoy the woods and the beauty, and the sunshine that I hadn't seen too much of in Normandy.

Then I remembered Roland's hunting dogs, and suddenly the woods and the sunshine weren't so sweet. If the Normans had dogs with them, they'd know I'd ridden into the river, and they'd assume I'd crossed. They could easily cross, too, and the dogs would pick up my trail again. Then I'd be caught in just the situation I wanted to avoid—being chased in the woods. It occurred to me that maybe I should cross back to the east bank again.

But if they didn't bring dogs, they'd probably ride along the road there, and there I'd be. For a minute there, I didn't know what to do. Surely, though, they'd bring dogs. From what Arno had told me, they almost always hunted with dogs. And how else could they hope to track me?

I stayed on the west side for a half mile or so, long enough to be out of sight of the wharf while crossing. Then I rode back to the riverbank and into the water again. In three or four minutes we were back on the east side and on the road. And everything went perfectly fine for about five minutes.

That's when four men stepped out of the woods about fifty feet ahead of me. They weren't Roland's men; I'd never seen them before. They were grinning, but they didn't look friendly at all. All of them wore hauberks, helmets, and swords. Two held bows, slightly bent and with arrows on their bowstrings. A third carried shield and spear, in case I charged, I supposed. The fourth, wearing a tunic over his hauberk, seemed to be the leader. He carried a shield on one arm and a sword in his other hand.

Automatically I looked back over my shoulder and saw another four coming out of the woods behind me.

Eight of them! They were probably looking for bigger prey than me, but apparently I'd do for an appetizer. These didn't look at all like the clumsy ragged bandits I'd seen in Provence. They looked more like knights gone outlaw. I recalled then what Arno had told us: that Roland's father had been killed recently fighting river pirates. I wondered if that's what these were.

"Stop and dismount!" the leader shouted.

I had to act quickly or I'd be dead. I might be anyway. I stopped my horse, and as my feet hit the road, my blaster was out of my holster. I fired twice at the men ahead of me, leaping aside almost at the same instant, seeing the leader fall as I rolled into the weeds beside the road.

Bowstrings twanged both ahead and in back of me as I scrambled behind the nearest tree. I fired several quick blasts at the men to the rear as an arrow thudded into the tree next to me. Besides the leader, two of the bowmen were down, and one of the spearmen, who'd been charging me. The remaining four had melted into the woods on my side of the road, not as if they were ducking out, but like men getting ready to slip up on me through the trees.

What was the matter with these guys? I wondered. They should have been horrified by the blaster. That was another difference between Norman warriors, I told myself, and the ragged bandits of Provence. And if I stayed where I was, they were going to kill me.

Crouching, I moved ahead, and one leaned

partly out from behind a tree, aiming an arrow. I got off a shot that grazed the trunk, gouging bark and wood and human flesh as the arrow shot off into the forest canopy above. Another arrow flew by from in front of me, only inches wide, as if the archer had released too soon, perhaps startled by the blast. I hit the ground behind a big tree with smooth gray bark, and lay there for a moment. I couldn't see anyone, and the two guys behind me would be coming up, slowly and cautiously, I hoped.

I didn't remember how many charges were left in the blaster, so I holstered it and drew my stunner, thumbing it on full and wide beam. We were close enough now for it to do the job. Then I jumped up and ran in the direction the last arrow had come from.

The bowman heard me running and stepped out with another arrow ready, drawing the bowstring as he moved. I hit the ground skidding on my stomach, firing at the same time. I never saw the arrow; it passed over me, I guess. All I saw was the Norman fall against the tree next to him and slide to the ground. That accounted for the four that had been in front of me, so I got up and just kept running for another sixty or eighty feet.

Then, since nothing more had happened, I ducked behind a thick trunk, panting, and looked back in the direction I'd come from. As far as I knew, there still were two behind me. If I wanted to get back to my horse, I had to go in their direction. But I didn't know how close they were, so I clipped the stunner back on my belt and drew the blaster. With it in my hand I started back, crouched and ready to sprint or to fire. The road was only a few yards to my left, and it occurred to me to angle toward it in case they decided to take the horse and call it a day.

It was exactly the right thing to do. Two of them were carrying a third man, wounded, toward the horse, apparently to load him on it. They were civilized enough to try to help their wounded. So instead of jumping out and shooting, I stepped into the road with the blaster pointed in a two-handed grip, and called to them to turn around and leave.

They stopped, stared at me for a moment, and one of them said something to the other. Carefully, they laid their partner down, then abruptly jumped for opposite sides of the road. I shot one of them, really gutting him, and it was just too much for the other. For a few seconds I got glimpses of him running hard through the trees, getting out of there.

Then I was alone, except for the guy who was wounded. I walked over to him. He was still breathing, noisily, but he was unconscious, and bleeding quite a lot. The energy bolt had torn away most of his left shoulder, and the side of his chest was torn open. His left arm would probably have torn off if his friends hadn't laid it across his stomach before they picked him up. While I watched, the blood quit pumping out of the wound, and I figured he must be dead.

I didn't feel sick or anything like that, and I certainly didn't feel guilty—I didn't even feel sorry it had happened, exactly. But now that the fight was over, I just kind of felt—wretched. I'm not sure why. They were Normans, and Arno said that almost every Norman male of noble birth, and some of common birth, dreamed of being a knight, and a hero in battle. Fighting, he'd said, was the salt of life for them.

Well, getting killed went along with that kind of thing, but I felt pretty depressed anyway.

And if I hung around there, I told myself, I was likely to get killed, too. And I didn't want to kill potential allies to defend myself. I noticed the guy with the tunic lying nearby, and went over to him. The energy bolt had torn off his left leg just above the knee, and I tried not to look at it. I might want his tunic later, when it cooled off at night. The tunic wasn't bloody—the blood had run down past his feet—and I pulled it off.

Then I went and got my horse, which surprisingly hadn't run off in spite of all the blaster fire. He was probably within twenty feet of where I'd gotten off him. Apparently Normans train their horses as skillfully as they ride them.

Normans! I'd learned a lot about Normans recently, but today I'd *really* learned about Normans. They were treacherous, there was no arguing about that. But they were also nearly fearless—every bit as brave as Arno said they were. They hadn't even panicked in the face of modern weapons. From what I'd seen, they really might be able to take the Federation corvette after all.

Meanwhile, some of them wanted to kill me. I kicked my horse into a brisk canter. Maybe the dead pirates in and around the road would give Roland food for thought. I was sure it would Arno.

ELEVEN

After a little I let my horse slow to a brisk trot again, but we were still putting a lot of miles behind us. Then, before too many minutes, I became aware of a distant sound behind me. My scalp prickled: it was hounds! It could have been just a party of knights out hunting game, but somehow I was pretty sure that what they were tracking was me.

I'd come several miles since I'd fought the pirates, so Roland and his people must have found the bodies by then. Apparently it hadn't made that much difference to them, hadn't scared them off. What it probably had done was make them more watchful and dangerous than they would have been otherwise.

I kicked my horse into a canter once more. It looked like I was going to find out how far you could push a horse before he quit or went down. And how far I could push myself; I was really saddle sore by then. I didn't really worry about how much I could take, though. I'd take as much as I needed to, to get me wherever I was going.

That's when it occurred to me that I had no idea where I was going!

I knew that somewhere, not too far ahead, the hills ended—a couple of miles or maybe four or five. Then they'd give way to a broad flat valley. I remembered that from flying over it on my stormy first day in Normandy. The flat district had a lot of cleared farmland, especially near the river, and villages and castles. There were even two or three fortified towns along the river there. What would the locals make of someone dressed like I was, running a horse as hard as he could? They wouldn't have to be too smart to realize I was being chased by someone.

And who would be chasing me but knights? As far as I could tell, they were the authorities in this country. And with clothes like mine, I was neither knight nor monk nor priest. Which seemed to mean I had no standing, nor rights to amount to much. Would people just try to stop me, without cause, and hold me for whoever was chasing me?

I was running away from trouble, but I might also be running into it! Still, I told myself, I was better off running toward possible trouble ahead than waiting for the certain trouble that was chasing me. I dug my heels into my horse's flanks to get a little more speed from him.

The baying of the hounds got fainter, and after two or three minutes I couldn't hear them at all. I was leaving them behind again.

Then it occurred to me that if I were Roland, I wouldn't be riding behind the hounds—not on the road like this. I'd leave two or three men with them and gallop on ahead. The hounds might be half a mile or more behind me, but how near were the nearest riders? I decided to look backward every few seconds. If someone came in sight chasing me, I'd take a shot at his horse with the blaster. That would slow him down, even if I missed!

In a pinch I could always lie in wait, of course, shoot the first riders or dogs, and then take off again. But I didn't want to kill Roland or any of his men. I still wanted to make a deal with them. Somehow, I had to outwit them and stay free long enough for dad to pick me up.

About then I rounded a curve and there was a knight about two hundred feet ahead of me, riding my way. As soon as we saw each other, he lowered his lance and shouted for me to halt. When I kept coming, full tilt, he kicked his horse into a gallop and charged. I snatched my stunner off my belt and pointed it, then pressed the firing stud at about seventy feet, aiming at the animal. He went down skidding, sliding along on sheer momentum, throwing the knight over his head.

It must have really jarred and shaken the guy to go down like that, as well as totally surprising him. So you can imagine how surprised I was when he landed rolling and came up on his feet, pulling at his sword. But by that time I had passed him, and all he could do was yell after me as I looked back. The whole thing took about three or four seconds.

When I rounded the next bend in the road, about a half mile farther on, I could see another road ahead that came down out of the hills to the river, with a wharf at its foot. A small barge-like ferryboat was just pulling away with several mounted churchmen on it, one of them pretty fancily dressed. Two oarsmen stood one on each side, rowing from a standing position with one long oar apiece. A third stood in the stern, sweeping another long oar from side to side. They were headed for the wharf across the river, where the road began again.

It seemed like the right time to take a chance. I slowed to a trot. When I got to the wharf, the ferry was most of the way across. I rode my horse right off the wharf, as if I'd gotten onto the ferry. It was only a couple of feet drop into the water, which seemed to be about five feet deep there. I felt his hooves hit the bottom, but it was too deep for him to wade. He bobbed back up and started to swim, and I headed him diagonally downstream to make it look to the boatmen as if I were crossing. Meanwhile, I took advantage of the current. Then, when I was around the bend in the river, just ahead, I'd angle back toward the east side again instead of crossing.

The knights were supposed to think that I'd taken the ferry to the west side. So they'd swim their horses across, I hoped, and the hounds would start hunting around over there for my trail, which they wouldn't find because I hadn't crossed. The knights would probably question the ferrymen, and maybe they'd catch on then or maybe they wouldn't. At any rate, there'd be confusion, and hopefully they wouldn't think to look for me back on the east side.

Hopefully. I had to take chances or they'd catch me almost for sure. Meanwhile, I could hear the hounds again. If some of the knights were riding ahead of them, they might be getting close to the wharf. I prodded my horse to get him to swim faster, and wished I knew his name. Horses seemed a lot like gorms in personality; if I knew his name, I could use it to urge him on faster.

At last the bend cut me off from view of the ferry and wharf, and I steered him toward the east shore. Darry—I decided I'd give him a name, and Darry was the name of the gorm we'd had for a couple of years when I was a kid—Darry, still seeming as strong as ever, took me back across and up the bank, dripping. I rode along through the woods for a little while before returning to the road. I wanted to quit dripping, so I wouldn't leave a track of wet drips where anyone would notice them. Just in case.

While I was jogging along through the trees, the baying got louder upstream, then changed. After a minute or so it stopped. I guessed that maybe the knights and dogs were swimming the river to the west bank. Three or four minutes after that I could hear them again, but this time it sounded really different, sort of a confused barking. I decided it was time to take to the road again.

I held Darry to a brisk trot as we went. Where to now, I asked myself, and what next? I could hardly keep running forever. I'd only been running for—it was probably about two hours—but besides being chased by a squad of knights, I'd been attacked by river pirates or highwaymen or whatever they'd been, and by a knight I didn't even know, just riding along the road! This country was dangerous enough for the people who lived here; it was no place for someone like me.

How long would it take before dad came looking for me? He thought I was safe back in Roland's castle, or maybe unsafe back in Roland's castle, and he wouldn't know otherwise until tomorrow morning before dawn, when he met or failed to meet with Arno. Then he'd either have to risk hunting for me by daylight or wait until the night after next. In either case, I was going to get awfully hungry, if I were still alive.

And maybe Arno would put him off, tell him I was back at the castle, sound asleep. But I didn't believe dad would fall for that. He'd know that something was peculiar; Bubba would for sure, if he were there. Still, what could dad do? He still might not know I was out wandering around the country.

And suppose—suppose Roland figured out something to trick him and take over the cutter himself! But he'd never get away with that, no chance, unless Arno helped him.

If Arno were really smart, he'd meet with dad, tell him what actually had happened, and dump Roland. Then they could come and find me, and we'd go recruit some new baron, or some more independent knights and sergeants.

But that wasn't what I wanted. Time was

limited, and the quickest thing was to pull Roland into the mission. He was already convinced that we were for real and were the key to something he wanted. And I couldn't see any reason to believe that some other baron would be more reliable.

I was riding along worrying like that when Darry gave a little snort, and sort of shied, nervously. Instantly I was alert, looking all around. He speeded his pace a little. A moment later I saw Bubba come loping out of the forest behind us. He'd picked up the horse's fear, though, and didn't try to catch us. He just closed up to about fifty feet and kept his distance.

"Am I still being followed?" I called to him mentally.

It was impossible for him to go through the effort of talking while he was running, so he didn't answer verbally. But he kept his pace even and his eyes on mine, calmly. I was sure he'd do something more than that if there were immediate danger. So I reined Darry off the road and into the forest, where I stopped and tied the reins to a young tree. Then I trotted back myself to talk with Bubba, far enough from Darry that he wouldn't go frantic on me.

"What happened?" Bubba wanted to know.

I told him. Not in words—that was slower than I needed to be with him—but by just sort of running back through my consciousness the major events since I'd left the cutter that morning before dawn. I'd talked to Bubba that way before; when you're used to it, it goes pretty fast. This time it took about two minutes. Then I ran my chief worries by him.

"But if Roland and his knights have quit hunting for me," I finished, "then all I need to do is hang around until dark, while you go and tell dad to come get me."

I'd hardly thought it when he heard the hounds again. I didn't; they were still too far off. But Bubba did. "It sounds like they going to stay after you," he said. "You keep going, be careful. We find you sometime tonight. We fly along river. You stay near it, within mile if you can."

Then he turned and loped away up the slope. I hoped the hound pack didn't leave my trail to follow his. He was bigger and stronger, but even so, they'd kill him if they caught him.

They wouldn't, though, I decided. They'd surely been trained not to leave one trail for another. I went over to Darry and untied him, swung up into the saddle, and hurried back to the road. Somehow I felt confident now. With dad informed, the situation would be under control before midnight. All I needed to do was keep running and not do anything stupid.

I urged Darry to a canter again as I rode away, feeling actually cheerful in spite of a sound that could only be the hounds.

TWELVE

I didn't stay cheerful long, though—maybe
another couple of miles. By that time, three
things were happening. Darry was definitely
tiring, although that didn't worry me too much.
After all, the horses chasing us would be tiring, too. Probably worse than Darry was, because they'd started out way behind and
carried more weight. And as far as that was
concerned, the hounds had to be getting tired
and sore-footed by now.

Second, the river valley was getting wider,
and the hills alongside it less high and steep.
Any time now, I'd be in farming country again.
There'd soon be castles and travelers, and
knights.

The third thing was the good thing: I couldn't
hear the hounds anymore.

Anyway, about three or four miles after
Bubba had left, Darry pulled up lame, slowing to a limping jog. It was the left front hoof.

I got down to look at it, taking the leg by the cannon bone and fetlock joint and raising it. Then, half crouching, I rested the cannon bone on my thigh, just above the knee, the way Rainulf had done when he was filing the horse's hoof. There was a stone stuck in the softer part of the foot; that had to be the trouble.

I didn't know how to get it out. The only thing I could think of was to dig it out with my knife, and I was scared to do it. Darry might kick me into the middle of next week, or jump and just plain run away.

But I had to do something about it, so I led him a little way back into the woods and tied the reins to a small tree. Then I raised the hoof again, took out my knife, and as gently as I could I dug out the stone. Darry flinched, but he didn't kick or anything like that. The stone was sharp, and it left a painful-looking depression in addition to the little cut I'd made digging it out.

I put the hoof down and stood there for a few seconds, stroking his velvety nose and thinking that I hadn't properly appreciated him till then, just taken him for granted. He wasn't a machine of some kind, he was a living, breathing being. But now I could hear the baying again, so I got back into the saddle and started off. He still limped a little for a short way. Then his gait pretty much smoothed out, but I could still tell it wasn't the same as it had been. He was favoring the left foreleg slightly, and he was also definitely wearing out. He'd probably do all right after a while, if I took it easy enough on him. But I knew, from studying the care of gorms, that if I kept running him when his gait wasn't right, he'd probably pull up seriously lame.

So I slowed him to an easy trot.

Meanwhile, the guys chasing me were still coming, and inside a couple of minutes I could tell that the hounds weren't quite as far off as they had been. The knights' horses were probably tiring worse than Darry, but even if some of them fell back, others would keep coming. I needed to watch for any opportunity to change to another horse, or maybe a boat—anything like that.

Right after that I rode out into open farmland, newly cleared, with the rotting stumps still standing hip high amid the growing crop they call wheat on Fanglith. Ahead, the land along the road was mostly open fields. The woods were mainly off to the east now, and to the west along the river. The river here lay quite a way off to my left, flowing now through lower, wetter ground. Not too far ahead I could see the huts of some farmers. Less than a mile away stood a castle, back from the road a short distance. Like Roland's, its manor house was built on a mound.

It occurred to me briefly that maybe I could exchange horses there. But it would take too long, even if they'd agree. And they'd probably ask questions. I'd just have to keep going the way I was, and hope for the best.

The hounds' baying told me that going on was the only possible decision. I was feeling pretty anxious now. For better or worse, I pushed Darry to a gallop again. I needed to be out of sight ahead when my pursuers rode out of the woods.

At least no one came out from the castle to challenge me.

Not far past the castle I approached another crossroad. I slowed to a quick trot and put on the tunic I'd taken from the dead pirate. Then, without asking myself what I was doing, I turned onto the crossroad, riding down it toward the river, which here was a good half mile below the road I'd been on.

The river was an attraction to me—it seemed as if it should be my salvation. But up till then I just hadn't known what to do with it.

Ahead of me now, in the road between me and the band of riverside woods, there was a small herd of cattle, about twenty-five or thirty of them. The Fanglith version of cattle are smoother-coated, rangier, and more excitable than the cattle of Evdash, and they have wide horns. But they're really not so different from ours. They were being driven toward the river by two peasants on foot and a knight or sergeant on horseback, and leaving the road spotted with their soft and rancid-smelling droppings.

I slowed to an easy jog to press through the herd, and the cattle got out of my way, jostling each other and bellowing. It seemed to me that the hounds would probably lose Darry's scent where the cattle tracked over it, and that the strong smell of the cattle and their droppings might easily spoil the sensitivity of their noses for a while afterward.

At least I hoped it would. In fact, I was depending on it.

The cattle were repeatedly trying to turn back past the men, as if they wanted to go back where they'd come from. The horseman and peasants had their hands full trying to keep them going west. Being as busy as he was, the swearing knight only glanced briefly at me as I passed. The strangeness of my clothes was not conspicuous while I wore the tunic. I was trusting that he'd ignore me when I was by, and not watch where I went.

I just kept trotting right on to the river, and rode out into the water. It was wider and shallower here than it had been upstream. As Darry waded out, I glanced behind me toward the men with the cattle, a quarter mile back. They were paying no attention to me. As soon as the water was deep enough that Darry was swimming, I turned him downstream, angling toward the far side. We came out of the water a couple of hundred yards below the ford and rode up into the woods.

There I got down and led him, walking. He deserved the rest, and if I hadn't permanently lost my pursuers, I hoped they'd at least be confused and thrown off for a while.

I could hear the hounds clearly now. A couple of minutes later their even chorus broke into the confusion I'd hoped for, then lessened into isolated barking. A little later the barking became excited, and I heard one shrill with pain. I wondered if he'd been hooked by a steer.

It was tempting to climb on Darry again and take the opportunity to widen the gap. But I was determined to rest him, so I simply walked faster myself, my faithful horse plodding behind.

THIRTEEN

I was lucky. By the time I decided to get back on Darry again, a mile farther on, there were no more hound sounds to be heard. I guessed that Roland had given up, but I wasn't taking any chances. I kept going, though slowly now, and watchfully, in case someone with sharp eyes was still after me and had found my tracks. Meanwhile, it was clouding up again, beginning to look threatening.

Finally, the river woods ended, with cattle pastures extending to the shore. For quite a way the pastures were thick with tall tree stumps, fairly recent-looking at first and then older and more rotten. It looked as if the population was increasing and clearing more land. As I rode, it occurred to me to wonder if Bubba had gotten back to the cutter yet. I decided he couldn't have; he'd had a long way to go from where he'd left me.

At one point a bull trotted over to confront

us. When he decided to do more than threaten, I had to stun him to avoid being chased back the way we'd come from. From there I aimed Darry northwest, to get on a road I could see that ran parallel to the river on this side.

Before long I could see an extensive palisade in the distance, and around it clusters of low buildings. A town, I decided. Inside the palisade, seemingly near the center of the enclosed area, was one largish building with a square tower. From where I was, it seemed to be made of stone. Probably a church, I decided, a building dedicated to their god.

Meanwhile, there was actually some traffic on the road here. An occasional crude wagon lurched and bumped in the rutted tracks. Men drove cattle, and bands of a smaller animal called sheep which make an almost constant bleating noise. Occasionally, a farmer pushed a wheelbarrow heaped with vegetables, or walked along with a rod across his shoulders. Sometimes dead poultry hung from the rod by their feet—ducks, and larger, long-necked birds that I think are called geese. At other times, baskets dangled.

I also met a few men on horseback, most of them apparently not knights, though every one of them carried a sword. None of them paid any attention to me. They were more interested in the heavy gray clouds, muttering and rumbling, that were moving in from the west. They had already cut off the early evening sun. I told myself it was going to be a wet night, and hoped dad would hurry. Meanwhile, I'd just have to take whatever came. A little rain couldn't hurt me.

Before long I came to the first buildings outside the palisade. The town seemed to have outgrown its wall, and was spilling out into the countryside. Some of the houses were made of boards and some of bricks. Their steep slanting roofs were thick bundles of long grass, laid down overlapping to shed the rain. And they'd soon have their chance: The great rumbling storm cloud, pulsing with lightnings, was almost overhead, moving fast, and the evening was suddenly getting dark before its time. A cold breeze whisked around us while the thunder boomed nearer.

The road entered the gates of the town. I'd liked to have gone in and looked it over, but somehow I felt uncomfortable about doing it. Besides, inside was not a good place for dad to pick me up. Another road circled the palisade not far outside, and I followed it instead.

I'd traveled it only a little way when I heard a roar approaching swiftly, a roar that was not thunder. Hailstones, mushy but big, began to spat down, followed moments later by a deluge of them as the roar was upon me. Suddenly, as if it had been saving itself for this, lightning flashed and stabbed. Thunder banged and crashed so close that my heart almost stopped, and Darry jumped, nearly throwing me. I found myself galloping toward the nearest house. Eaves that overhung its front, and the separate roof over the front entrance, were no protection at all. The wind drove a great mass of soft hail splattering against the wall and us as I banged demandingly on the door.

A middle-aged man opened it a crack, a sword in his fist. For just a moment he stared, then shouted over the roar of the storm to go around back. I did. He was waiting for me at the back door, a hooded cloak thrown over him, and led me on a run to an adjacent shed. There I took the bit from Darry's mouth, and the man replaced his bridle with a halter, tying him while I removed the saddle. Then he handed me a sack and took another himself, and we rubbed the horse down. When we were done, he nodded to me.

There was another horse in the shed, a smaller, older animal that didn't look nearly as good as Darry. There was also a small stack of hay. Apparently this man couldn't afford a barn with a hay loft, but bought hay now and then as needed. He took a crude-looking two-tined pitchfork and piled some of the hay in a manger where Darry could eat it.

When he had done that, he nodded to me again, and we walked to the door of the shed. So far, neither of us had spoken since his shouted order at the front door. Together we looked out. The ground was covered with two inches of slush and ice. The hailstones falling now were hard, and an inch thick, huge armies of them booming against the walls, bouncing and popping. He closed the door again and turned to me.

"The hail will stop soon enough," he said, and shook his head. "I don't think I've ever seen it come down so hard, and I've lived forty-four summers in this life." He looked me over curiously, his eyes taking in the unusual cut of the pants and boots that he could see below my tunic. "Where do you come from, and what is your business here?"

"I'm from a distant land," I said, "called Morn Gebleu. I'm in Normandy looking for my parents, and they are here looking for me. I have hope that the good god will bring us together, perhaps tonight." With that I crossed myself the way the locals did.

He crossed himself, too. "May it happen as you wish. Are you able to pay for a night's lodging?"

"No sir," I said. "But if I may stay here in the shed until the hail stops, I'll be on my way."

He shook his head. "No need. Your horse looks truly worn out, and you'll need to eat. If you could pay, I'd ask it, but I'll not turn you out on a night like this for lack of a copper or two. Come. It sounds like the hail has turned to rain now. We can run to the house with no more than a wetting, and dry our clothes before the fire. And my wife has a thick stew ready at this moment."

He threw open the door and we ran for it.

I really was hungry, and tired, too. When we had finished eating, we sat around and talked for a while, the man and I, his wife, and their thirteen-year-old daughter. They also had a grown son, whom the town magistrates employed as a guardsman. He would be home at midnight.

The man's name was Pierre, and he owned and operated a nearby tannery. I didn't know what a tannery was, but figured I'd better not ask. It might be something I'd be expected to know already. Anyway, they were good people, friendly, and frequently called upon the good Jesus and the gentle Mary, two principal figures in their religion.

Meanwhile, the bug bites I'd gotten the night before in Roland's castle were itching. All afternoon I'd been too busy to notice them much. Now I was trying not to scratch in front of my host and hostess, although I noticed them scratching now and then.

After a little while I was having a hard time staying awake, itch or no itch. They offered me a bag of hay to sleep on, but I wanted to sleep in the shed, where dad could get me without waking anyone. I couldn't tell them that, of course, so I told them I didn't want to be separated from my horse that long. Apparently that sounded reasonable to them, because they didn't say anything more about the bag of hay.

By that time, the storm had become just a moderate rain. The wife handed me a woolen cloak for a blanket, and I sprinted to the shed. Night was almost there by then, and inside the shed it was almost pitch dark when I closed the door, so I opened it enough to see by while I made a bed out of some of the hay.

I told myself that dad might be overhead right now, getting ready to land. But he might also be drinking a hot cup of korch and wondering how Arno and I were doing with Roland. Bubba might just now be trotting out of the woods into the opening. At any rate, I was too tired to sit up waiting; they could wake me when they got there. I lay down, closed my eyes, and the last thing I remember doing as I went to sleep was scratching my leg with my other heel.

FOURTEEN

It didn't seem like I'd slept very long when someone shook me. I woke up wide awake, thinking it must be dad, but there was torch-light, and it was Pierre's face that looked down at me. I could see he was worried about something, and that really wakened me.

"What is it?" I asked, sitting up.

"Guillaume, my son, came home, and I woke up. He told me the magistrates are looking for a foreigner, and from the description, I am sure it is you. All the guards will be watching for you, so you must be well away from here before daylight. Also, there are men watching the road. You are supposed to be very danger-ous, and are to be turned over to the young Baron Roland de Falais, whom you are said to have robbed.

"No one believes the baron, but he is a man of influence with the duke. He was a champion in the duke's great victory at Hastings, and the duke is a man whose good will is important to the town, so it will be as the baron wishes.

"My son is asleep now, but you must leave at once." Then he added, "The rain has almost stopped."

I got up and handed Pierre the cloak his wife had given me. "Are they watching the road around the town, too?"

He nodded. "I am sure they would watch that. Yes."

I knew then what I was going to do. "Look," I said, "the horse is not mine. I was being held hostage by Roland, and took it to escape. I leave it with you. You can keep it if it's safe to, or you can turn him out to wander until someone claims him as a stray. I'll travel by foot."

"By foot at night? It is not safe!"

"For me," I said, "nothing is safe. And thank you for your kindness." I crossed myself. "May the good god bless you."

He looked soberly at me and didn't say anything more as I said goodbye to Darry and left.

The rain had slackened a lot since I'd gone to bed, though the clouds kept it really, really dark. But it still made enough faint sound to reduce what a person could hear, which was both an advantage and a disadvantage. Meanwhile, the combination of weather and the late hour meant that hardly anyone would be out and around. If I saw anyone, I could be suspicious of them, and vice versa.

I could barely make out the town palisade about two hundred feet away, and oriented myself by it. The river would be to my right, and I turned that way. What I'd do was follow it toward the sea, which couldn't be too terribly far away. The chances were that dad would be along any time now, but if for some reason he didn't show up tonight, I'd hole up somewhere and wait for him.

I started picking my way eastward between the somewhat scattered buildings. You'd think I'd have been barked at by some of the local canids, or even harassed by them, but there didn't seem to be any. I wondered if there were enough hungry people around that canids got killed and eaten, or whether they were all indoors and just didn't notice me, quiet as I was.

It seemed to me that once I got well away from the town, I ought to be safe from the baron. Ten knights and sergeants wouldn't stretch very far—not even the sixteen he'd have if Arno was cooperating with him in this. And I didn't think he'd notify the other barons. They'd be curious about me if he did, and if one of them got me, Roland would probably never see me or my weapons again. Probably no one else would, either; Roland would have figured that out. And the town guards would only be watching for me around town.

To keep from getting too chilled, I started jogging. I went as light-footedly as I could, to avoid the sound of splashing, and continued to stay away from the road. It was hard to believe that men would be out in the open watching on a night like that, but it was no time to take needless chances. I kept my eyes open for sign of anyone at all.

If anyone challenged me, I'd be very obedient until they were close enough to stun. I didn't feel like I was in too much actual danger, with the weapons I had on my belt. But I wanted to stay free and get picked up by dad while still keeping it possible to make a deal with Roland. So I definitely didn't want to kill any of his men, although it occurred to me that he might easily forgive the loss of a man or two if it came down to grabbing some power.

It only took four or five minutes of jogging before I could see the river just ahead of me. The palisade was still in sight to my left, and from where I was, it seemed to go right down to the river. To go downstream past the town, I'd need to take to the water and swim past it.

Fine, I thought. I knew from experience that the water wasn't too cold. The combination of weapons, communicator, jumpsuit, and tunic wouldn't help my buoyancy any, but I was sure I could do it.

Then I stopped, suddenly, and lowered myself to the wet ground. Out on the water, not far from shore, I'd seen movement, something floating down the current. I watched it float past me, less than a hundred feet away, a small boat with men in it. It made my hair crawl. Somehow it seemed to me they weren't just casual boatmen, not just travelers caught out in the weather and returning late to town.

When I couldn't see them anymore, I went quietly to the bank, slid down it, and stepped into the water. Within three steps it was over my head, and I let the current take me, swimming on my side enough to move out farther from shore.

But not too far. Not too far to see what was going on along the riverside. The palisade didn't go quite to the river. It went down near the river, to the top of a river terrace that stood a few feet above the flood plain. Then it turned and went along the top of the terrace, maybe twenty feet back from the bank, enclosing the town on the side toward the river. I could understand that. Why build it on a flood plain?

Pretty much the whole riverbank there seemed to be built up with timbers to serve as a long wharf. Several low ships were tied up to it, none of them more than thirty or maybe forty feet long, I suppose. At least a couple of them had single masts that I could see dimly in the night. The current would take me by them about twenty feet out.

And I saw what the boatmen were up to. They had pulled up alongside one of the ships there, tying to her gunwale, and as I drifted toward them, I saw them climb over the side onto the ship. Thieves, I thought. It didn't make sense that they were sailors who belonged aboard her. They were there to rob the ship, I felt sure.

I don't remember deciding to do what I did next. It seems as if I just did it. Actually it's as if I watched myself doing it. I changed the direction of my stroke to take me in closer to the shore and the ship, at the same time assuring myself that everything would work out just fine. In half a minute I had hold of the skiff they'd come there in.

The skiff, about ten feet long, was tied to a big thole pin, which told me this ship could be rowed. The ship's side rose only about forty inches out of the water, and pulling myself up with the skiff's rope, I grabbed the gunwale.

I could hear voices talking in undertones—little more than whispers. It sounded as if they were on the other side of the ship, and toward the bow. Ever so quietly I untied the skiff and let myself slide back into the water. The current carried it away downstream, with me holding on to her rope. When they went to load their loot, they'd discover her gone, but by that time I'd be out of sight and out of reach. And they'd be stuck there. Served them right.

When I couldn't see the ships anymore, I worked myself back to the rear of the skiff and climbed aboard her there, where she wouldn't tip over with me. She had oars, shipped under the middle seat, and thole pins set in the gunwales to brace the oars for rowing. It was the perfect solution to going down the river.

And it felt good to row a boat again, the first time since I'd left Evdash. I'd just row along until dad came, staying close enough to the shore that I could get to it quickly when I saw him.

After an hour or so, though, I'd had more than enough rowing, and decided to just drift with the current. I was starting to get blisters. There was a paddle on board as well, and I just sat in the stern, using it as a tiller while I watched the darkness slide by. The rain had stopped, except for some drizzle off and on. When I'd get a little sleepy, or a little too chilly, I'd do pushups off the center seat to warm up and get wider awake.

Somehow it didn't seem safe to go to sleep on board, and I didn't want to go ashore yet. I felt safer out on the river, and if dad didn't pick me up tonight, then I wanted to get by as many towns and castles as possible before daylight. What I really preferred, if I didn't get picked up, was to get all the way to the sea.

Finally though, the first tinge of dawn began to gray the sky, and I could see a little farther. The river was wider here. In a few minutes, up ahead, I could make out the stone castle I'd noticed when we'd first seen the River Orne. I was almost to the sea.

It occurred to me then that it might not be too smart to go out to sea in a flat-bottomed skiff. As I got closer, I could see near the castle a village with a palisade, so I took the oars and rowed toward a woods on the opposite side of the river.

It was beginning to rain again as I pulled the skiff ashore. And I was really pretty tired. So I dragged it up to where the ground wasn't so muddy, turned it over, and crawled underneath. If I had to sleep cold, at least I wouldn't have the rain falling on me.

I'm not sure how long I slept—maybe three or four hours. It was voices that woke me. Not mom's and dad's speaking Evdashian, but men's speaking Norman.

"It's ours, all right," said one. "I told you I recognized it."

"See!" said a second. "I told you I tied it up good! There ain't no way it could have got up here by itself. Someone stole it, sure as hell!"

I should have realized what was going on, but I was still fuzzy-minded from sleep. Before I thought to reach for my stunner, the boat was turned over, they saw me lying there, and one of them jumped on me. I didn't struggle. All it would have earned me was a beating, or maybe a cut throat. Hand-foot art didn't occur to me at the moment, and it has its limits anyway. Particularly when you're on your back and there are three of them.

The guy who jerked me to my feet wasn't very big, but his strength had a fierceness to it. Another grabbed me from behind. One of them had pulled a long knife from a sheath and held it to my throat.

"Careful with that," said the one who seemed to be the leader. "The captain will want to talk to him. Hold it up to him, to make sure he behaves himself, but don't draw blood unless he struggles."

Silently I thanked the man, and promised myself I wouldn't struggle. I'd be very well behaved until I had a chance to do something effective and hopefully not too risky. Meanwhile, they paid no attention to my weapons; obviously, it never occurred to them what they were.

Two of them frog-marched me to the edge of the water, where there was a roundish sort of little boat, of leather stretched over a frame of saplings, with paddles in it. The other one dragged the skiff down. "We'll all ride the skiff," the leader said, "and tow the Breton coracle."

Anchored eighty feet offshore, I could see what looked to be the ship of the night before, the one I'd taken the skiff from. "Just a minute!" I said, staring at it. "How did that get here?" I was talking more to myself than to them.

"The *Jeanette Louise*?" the leader said. "We rowed her. How does a crew usually move a ship on a river?"

A crew! And these men were part of it. Aboard her I could see another twelve or fifteen men, and there might be more out of sight below the gunwales. It occurred to me that I had made a serious mistake the night before. "Wait," I said. "Last night I saw some men climb aboard that ship from this skiff. Was that you?"

"Aye, we were two of them, Charles and me."

"And you were whispering as if you were sneaking."

"We were whispering. It would be worth a fist in the face to wake our captain. Why do you ask these questions?"

"You'd never believe me," I said. I'd really blown it, I told myself. I'd jumped to a conclusion and gotten myself into a situation I'd never be able to talk my way out of. The man behind me twisted my arm higher behind my back as another pushed the skiff into the water. While two of them steadied it, the other one walked me to the bow and pushed me to my knees. The others pushed off the shore. One of them took the oars and began to row, while by now some thirty or so heads were watching from the little ship.

I wondered why it took so many men to row something no larger than that—thirty feet long at the most. Maybe, I thought, these weren't innocent merchant seamen after all.

We were there in less than a minute. Two of the men on the ship reached over the gunwales to yank me up by the arms and dump me sprawling on the deck. But it still wasn't time to go for my stunner, because two others grabbed me as soon as I'd landed, to jerk me back onto my feet. They turned me half around, and I found myself facing the captain. I was pretty sure that's who it was, because of the richer-looking, more colorfully dyed clothes he wore.

"A thief!" he said grinning at me, and rubbed his hands together. "Would you like to know how we handle such as you?"

"Sir." I answered. "You'll never find a better recruit than me if you live to be a hundred. There's not many with the nerve to steal the skiff off a ship like this one."

His eyebrows raised. "Oh?" He looked me over. "A recruit? You're big enough and to spare," he said, "and that's a fact. Where did you get those clothes?"

"Off the back of one who didn't need them any longer."

He pursed his lips and cupped his chin in one hand, his hard eyes searching mine. I gave him look for look.

"And how did you manage that? You carry no arms."

"I did then."

"What happened to them?"

"The guardsmen took them."

"The guardsmen. Hmm. I suppose you'll tell us now that you broke free from the guardsmen."

By that time the crew was standing around grinning. They weren't taking me seriously anymore—I was just a fool trying to bluff his way out of getting killed. The man holding my arms from behind had relaxed his grip a little. The man who'd held his knife to me earlier was just now climbing over the gunwale, the last aboard.

I struck the man behind me in the groin with a "spike hand" at the same instant I stomped hard on his instep, then spun with a "cleaver hand," knocking him to the deck. My stunner was in my fist before anyone reacted, and I swung it around with the stud depressed. Several men went down, including the captain, and several others staggered, but mostly they just stood, astonished. I knew at once what the problem was; I'd just used up the charge.

I didn't wait around to explain. And I didn't have a fresh charge, even if I'd had time to put it in. I took two quick steps, jumped, kicked off the top of the gunwale and dove into the river. I swam underwater quite a way, which wasn't as far as I should have, and surfaced, kicking and stroking hard for shore. I heard yelling behind me, and after a few seconds saw an arrow strike the water right next to me. I dove again, and this time didn't come up until the bottom shoaled be-

neath me by the shore. I burst splashing out
of the water and raced, gasping for air, across
the narrow beach into the woods. Behind the
first big tree I stopped and looked back, heav-
ing and shaking.

I could hardly believe I'd gotten there without arrows in my back. I suppose there'd been
no bows strung, and it had taken a minute
before more than one or two men had thought
to go for them. Now there were several men
in the skiff, one rowing and one in the stern
paddling hard.

I knew how to send them back: a shot into
the bow from the blaster. If that didn't do it, I
might have to shoot one of them. I raised the
pistol in a firm two-handed grip, aimed, and
squeezed the trigger. Nothing!

The only thing I could think of was that it
had leaked. They were supposed to be water-
proof, but somewhere, somehow, this one
leaked.

I turned and began to jog through the trees.
I still hadn't gotten my wind back from swimming under water, and I hadn't done any running to speak of since we'd left Evdash. But I
was sixteen, and probably still a better runner than guys who only had a thirty-foot ship
to walk and run on. At rowing, any of them
could beat me without sweating, but in a foot
race . . .

I looked back. The boat had landed, I could
tell, because through the trees I glimpsed two
guys running after me. I speeded up. Maybe
some of them were pretty good runners after
all. And I recalled now that, in boat racing at
home, the oarsmen pushed hard with their

legs on each stroke. It hadn't been my sport, but I could see that maybe their legs, and even their lungs, might be in pretty good shape after all.

Then, ahead of me, I saw through the trees an open field. I speeded up some more. If the guys behind me were carrying bows, I needed to be across the opening before they got to it, or at least as far ahead of them as possible.

I was very nearly sprinting when I came to the opening, and never looked back till I got to the forest on the other side. They were still coming, but those who were running across the field weren't carrying bows. They carried short swords in their hands—dangerous enough, but not at a hundred feet.

The ground began to climb here, but I kept running. I lost track of them then. Gasping and sweating, legs rubbery, I kept going, not running very fast any longer, but never stopping. In places it got kind of steep, and sometimes I had to scramble on all fours. I didn't know whether they were still after me, but what I had to do, it seemed to me, was keep going until I absolutely couldn't run another step. By then they should have given up and gone back.

I did, and they had. At least as far as I could tell they had. Maybe they'd given up when they couldn't catch glimpses of me anymore. Maybe they weren't able to track me.

After a few minutes collapsed on the ground, I sat up and looked around. I was on top of a plateau, in a tiny opening in the forest where bedrock came to the surface and there was almost no soil for trees to root in. The trees around it were small, and there was little undergrowth except for thin grass.

I was on a tableland, near the cliffs that went down to the beach. Even sitting there I could look out through the trees and see the gray sea, stretching to the edge of viewing. It had begun to rain again, a cooling rain that felt good on my sweaty body. And the sky looked as if it might start raining hard at any time.

My mind began to work again. With a sky like that, dad could fly. And certainly Bubba must have reached him by now. They'd be somewhere up there looking for me. I needed to find an opening big enough for them to land in.

After another minute I got up and began to walk. I didn't know what the best direction was, but I knew that sometimes the soil is thinnest near the edge of cliffs. So I kept walking along near the edge. After a little while I came to a narrow ravine, cliff-sided, not much more than a crevice. Looking over the edge, I could see a tiny brook down in the bottom, probably courtesy of the wet summer.

I turned and followed the edge southward until I came to the head of the ravine. It was steep, but not as rugged as the one I'd found as a possible hiding place for the cutter, so I started picking my way downward. After some climbing and scrambling, I came to a pool of clear water and got down on my knees to drink. I really swilled it down; I'd sweated out a lot of water being chased.

Not many minutes later I reached the beach, but I didn't go out on it. Instead, I stayed in the mouth of the ravine, beneath the cover of some scrubby trees there. I knew if I lay down, I'd go to sleep, and I remembered what had happened the last time I went to sleep. But then I told myself that it was dumb to feel that way. Just because I'd gotten into trouble one time didn't make it dangerous ever to sleep again.

So I lay down and closed my eyes. When I opened them the next time, Bubba was standing beside me, grinning.

FIFTEEN

The cutter was on the beach, right at the mouth of my little ravine, with the ramp out, waiting for us. Boy, you can't imagine how great it was to go aboard her! I didn't feel a bit tired, either! Dirty, wet, and all messed up, but not tired. Mom gave me a big hug, while dad stood behind her, nearly grinning his face in two. Then he shifted us down the beach a way and parked in the ravine I'd found the first day. I spent the next couple of hours telling them what happened to me and finding out what had been going on with them.

And eating, of course. Mom had arranged with Arno, a couple of times, to bring local foods when he came to report. So I had sliced pig meat and eggs, and coarse toasted bread from one of the local grains, with the local version of butter. Frankly, I can't tell the local eggs from what we have on Evdash, and the butter isn't much different, or the bread, as far as that's concerned. But pig meat is something special. It's kind of like kliss, but even more flavorful.

Anyway, what had delayed their finding me was some Norman knights out hunting. Bubba had been halfway to the cutter when their dogs had spotted him and cut him off. They'd chased him all over the countryside and nearly caught him. The hunting dogs operated like a team with their knights, and they knew the country thoroughly. While they were on his trail, he'd had to pretty much forget about the cutter. It took all his attention to escape alive. Several times he'd been very close to getting killed by the dogs or by arrows.

Finally though, when they saw the storm rolling in, the knights had blown their hunting horns, calling in their dogs, and headed for home. It had hailed there, too, and Bubba had taken shelter beneath the uptilted roots of a partially fallen tree that was hung up in a larger one. It had been well along toward dawn when he finally got to the cutter's hiding place, and by then, dad had shifted to the meeting place not far from Roland's castle.

So poor Bubba, tired and footsore, had made the five-mile run there, arriving just as the cutter was disappearing into the clouds again. Dawn was starting to break, and no one had come out to meet them. That meant another five miles back to the little meadow again for Bubba. He'd walked most of the way; he hadn't had much run left in him.

It sounded to me as if his previous twenty hours had been at least as wild and dangerous as mine had been, and a lot more strenuous.

When at last Bubba dragged himself up the ramp, he told mom and dad what had been going on with me. He also said he'd never been so tired before in his whole life. He'd never even imagined being so tired.

Now, though, we had to get back on the track and make some progress on Project Deneen. And dad agreed with me: What we needed to do next was go back and make a deal with Roland. He might be a criminal mentally, but we didn't really see any other choice. And it seemed as if right then was the time to do it. We needed to make contact again before Arno left Roland's castle, if he hadn't already. And while the cloud layer wasn't thick any longer, at least it hadn't started to break up.

So dad lifted again to two miles, which was up in the clouds, and returned to the coordinates of Roland's castle. Then he set slowly down right in the bailey, right in front of the entrance of the manorhouse. Someone must have seen us early and started yelling, because as we lowered, people were running every which way, headed for the nearest or strongest cover. And let me tell you, no one came out, but no one! Not even a hound! The only things moving around were some ducks, geese, and pigs, and even they stayed well away. It was as if the whole place had a guilty conscience and was afraid of us.

Also, they were probably remembering what had happened to the gate, which hadn't been replaced yet, and they'd probably all heard about the dead river pirates.

We didn't do a thing, just waited for them

to make the first move. After about five minutes, Father Drogo came out. He walked to about fifteen feet from us, made the sign of the cross, and stopped. I spoke to him with the loud-hailer, the volume turned down low. It seemed to me that just now the most effective approach was to be aloof. They'd probably have more respect for me unseen within the persteel sides of the cutter than as an unarmored kid.

"Is the Baron Roland de Falais still interested in the proposal that was made to him yesterday?" I asked.

I couldn't read Father Drogo's expression. All he said was, "I will see." Then he turned and went back in the house, closing the door behind him.

I hoped the priest wasn't mad about yesterday. (Was it only yesterday? So much had happened since then!) He was the most decent person there, as far as I could see. I mean, I liked Arno, but I really couldn't see him taking a serious risk for me without any apparent profit in it for himself, the way Drogo had.

About a minute later, Roland appeared, with Arno on one side of him and Drogo on the other. Through the loud-hailer, I repeated my question: "Is the Baron Roland de Falais still interested in the proposal that was made to him yesterday? If he says no, we shall not offer it to him again. We will invite Sir Arno to come with us, and we will take it elsewhere."

I felt pretty good about that as I said it. It felt like just the right thing to say. And his answer was a start in the right direction. "I

will be happy to ally myself with your lordship," he said. "That is, if this knight"—he
indicated Arno—"can come to an agreement
with me on leadership and the division of
spoils."

I raised the volume of the loud-hailer a bit,
to stress that I was the boss here now. "Leadership is for me to assume or assign as I see
fit," I replied calmly. "And almost a fortnight
ago I chose Sir Arno to gather and lead the
Norman force. As for the spoils, I have no
interest in that. You do not need an agreement between you yet concerning spoils. I
doubt you would keep such an agreement anyway, considering the treachery you undertook
yesterday. Divide the spoils when you have
them in hand.

"Meanwhile, I am impatient. Make up your
mind whether you will be a great lord who
commands great armies or a petty lord weep-
ing in his beer over the opportunity he let slip
away! Swear fealty to me now, until the enemy warship is ours and my sister is back in
my hands, or we will leave."

When I'd finished, I could hardly believe it
had been me talking! Larn kel Deroop Rostik,
age sixteen, of Carlinton Middle School! I was
so taken with my own clever eloquence that I
almost missed Roland's answer.

"Very well, my lord," he said. "I do so swear,
on the name of our Blessed Savior, in the
witness of this priest and this knight."

I remembered then one of the things Brother
Oliver had told me: If a knight swears an oath
on the Savior or his Blessed Mother, or even
on a saint, he will almost certainly keep it,

although he may twist it nearly beyond recognition. I felt as if we had an agreement now that could work, but I'd still have to watch out for him.

And it occurred to me that I'd had no such oath from Arno! We'd just sort of gone along on a gentlemen's agreement! But I wouldn't ask for an oath from him in front of Roland. That would have to wait until we were alone. Otherwise, the baron would think I was stupid for not getting one sooner.

What we did next was agree where Arno and Roland would go next in recruiting. I explicitly put Arno in charge of that, too. Roland obviously wasn't too happy about it, but he didn't argue. I suspected that, if and when they had a corvette in their hands, one of them would give the other the ax, or maybe a dagger under the ribs.

But meanwhile, it actually looked as if they'd both pull more or less together up to that point.

SIXTEEN

It took Arno only three more castles—five more days—to get his recruits up to thirty-three. He did it without any more personal appearances from me, too. Roland's presence with him was a big help. Roland already had a reputation as someone with a nose for politics and profit, a man who would someday be rich and powerful. He'd been close to Duke William, then had shown the good sense to come back to Normandy as one of the duke's loyal supporters at home instead of staying in England under the great man's thumb.

Arno reported the final recruits just before dawn on the sixth morning. He also told me that Roland had been very agreeable—had hardly argued about anything since I'd gotten his oath. That sounded promising, as if we'd be able to work with him without worrying too much that he'd do something crazy and unexpected.

We agreed it was time now to try for a chaser. I corrected myself mentally before I said it out loud: not *try*—it was time to *capture* a chaser.

That day we flew by daylight again, in spite of a clear sky, to select a place to set up the action. All our troops were at Roland's castle now, so we decided on a little one-room log hut not too far from it, where forest bordered on a big meadow near the edge of Roland's fief. A herdsman lived there, one of Roland's villeins, tending cattle. I told Arno to have Roland remove the cattle from the area of the herdsman's hut before evening, so they wouldn't be wandering around in the way, complicating things.

Then we sat a quarter-mile above the hut and talked about how we were going to pull it off. Three civilians, almost unarmed, one of them a sixteen-year-old and another one his mother, were going to capture a Federation corvette that was parked a few hundred miles above the planet! And they were going to do this with the help of some thirty primitive barbarians armed with swords. Barbarians who were looking for the chance to cut each other's throats, and maybe ours, too.

It didn't pay to look at it like that, I decided. I could feel my confidence shrinking when I did, and I didn't have too much to begin with.

You could hardly call what we did planning; there were too many unknowns to plan much. But we talked about how we'd deploy to start things out. After that we agreed on a few simple steps that were supposed to lead to success, accomplishing these any way we could. What it really came to was, we'd do whatever the situation called for, and hope for the best.

I was beginning to feel pretty tense, but Arno didn't seem nervous at all. Maybe that was because he was a Norman, with the idea that he could do anything.

Finally, we flew Arno and his horse back to Roland's castle and set him down right in the bailey. It was the first look that the new men had had at the cutter. And it was good public relations for Arno, getting taxied around like that. He was the only Norman who had flown, and no one could doubt that he was really number one with us.

For the rest of the day, about all we had to do was wait—dad and mom and I. Bubba ran off to gather his wolves. I lay down, but for once I couldn't go to sleep right away. While I lay there, I couldn't help thinking about the possibility of failure, and that we might be stranded here on this planet.

If that happened, I'd have some decisions to make. First, what would I do on Fanglith? Maybe I could train to be a knight. I shouldn't be too old to learn. Back on Evdash I was considered strong for my age and size, and an outstanding natural athlete. And it seemed to me that I could not only get through the knight training, but be very good at it, even if I would be starting late.

But then what? I didn't have any interest at all in going into battle and killing people, and that's what the knight business was all about. Not that they seemed to think of it as the knight *business*. It was a way of life that they followed, for whatever reason. Maybe because it was better than anything else on Fanglith, or on this part of Fanglith anyway.

What might my reasons be for becoming a knight? Why did knight training appeal to me if I didn't want to be a warrior? I decided it was because it would be great to be that good at something. Those little kids I'd seen training were going to be super-expert warriors.

But being super expert wasn't quite it either, for me. That was close, but it wasn't it. The training would be kind of a game, too—not in the sense of a contest against anyone, but a kind of— It would let me find out how good I could get at operating my body and having it perform really difficult things.

And controlling my mind! There was the secret of the champion distance runner, weight lifter, gymnast, and maybe the mathematician. Or someone like dad—the top-flight management consultant. The same would be true of knighthood—getting so good at something that nothing mental got in your way. These knights never worried about combat techniques. They were so good at them, it was all automatic. They could give their whole attention to the battle situation.

But as a knight, the real test was combat. They didn't even get to be knights until they'd impressed their officers by acts of valor in real combat. Arno had been tested in Sicily, first in some skirmishes, and finally, in a big battle. And Roland had been a bloody battle hero in England. But I didn't want to kill anyone if I could help it—certainly not just to show how good I was at fighting. And I definitely didn't want anyone to kill me, which was the other side of that coin.

Next, I looked at the possibility of being a monk or a priest. It wouldn't be so bad if I could be like Brother Oliver. He had something that the other monks I'd talked with, and Father Drogo, didn't. He had enthusiasm. He *loved* being a monk and knowing all the stuff he knew about his religion. And about a lot of other stuff. I couldn't have that enthusiasm because the stuff there was to know about his religion was mostly not real to me. It was interesting, and maybe I could get into sorting and analyzing it for what truths it did hold. But no, I wouldn't be happy as a monk or priest. I'd need to believe, first.

Maybe I'd need to see some more of Fanglith, and see what other options there were. But, of course, what I really needed to do was make this project work. I needed to get Deneen back from the political police, and head out for someplace like Evdash.

And then I'd still have to find out what I wanted to do.

Things like that went on in my mind for quite a while, but finally I went to sleep.

When the sun had gone down and it was starting to get dark, I flew the cutter into the woods behind the hut. That may sound strange, but it was easy. Cattle had grazed in that woods, apparently for a lot of years, and they'd eaten all the new tree seedlings as they came up. So there weren't any thickets or saplings or young trees at all, just the stand of big trees, with grass underneath. That left plenty of room between the trunks to float the cutter in, and once in there, we were practically impossible to see from above.

I set the cutter on the ground about a hundred yards back in the woods, beneath the spreading crown of a huge old tree. I wasn't feeling very well. My stomach was nervous and my skin felt numb, and I felt kind of weak all over. I had this growing premonition that the whole thing was going to be a disaster. If I'd been able to think of any other possible way to get Deneen back, I'd have left right away.

The knights and sergeants were already there, most of them sitting on their horses, talking. They seemed entirely relaxed and alert; it was awesome how unworried they were. Arno and Roland were with them. I didn't know if Bubba had arrived with his wolves or not, but then, I didn't know what they'd be able to do anyway. If they were around, they'd stay out of sight. Otherwise the knights would go after them and try to kill them.

I got out of the cutter with a blast rifle slung on one shoulder, and talked with Arno for a few minutes, letting it get darker. Then I went to the hut. There were four knights waiting around outside it with bows and arrows, to back me up when the chaser got there.

The poor herdsman was inside the hut. He'd been ordered to stay when the cattle had been driven away, and he didn't have any idea what was going on. He just hunkered in a corner of the hut, keeping quiet and out of the way.

It wasn't dark enough yet by quite a bit, so I walked back to the cutter to do my waiting.

I wondered if I looked as jittery to the knights as I felt. In the cutter, nobody said much. Mom had heated a pot of korch, and I had a cup.

I'd never noticed before how long it took to get dark.

We heard a kind of low plaintive howl from far back in the forest, and decided it was Bubba calling, so dad left to go back and see what he had to tell us.

It was about ninety percent dark when I got out and walked to the hut once more. I was so nervous I could hardly breathe. It was nearly time, and I didn't want to wait any longer. I took the communicator off my belt and spoke into it.

And suddenly I wasn't nervous anymore.

"This is Klentis kel Deroop," I said, "calling the Federation police corvette." I tried to make my voice sound weak and feverish. "I'm hiding in an abandoned hut down here, by a pasture. Are you getting my coordinates? I've been shot with an arrow, and the wound is badly infected. I'm afraid if I don't get medical attention right away, I'll be dead by tomorrow."

There was a long wait, maybe a minute, I suppose while they waited for the captain to come to the radio. Finally a voice, very businesslike, said, "Comrade kel Deroop, we have your coordinates. A chaser will be there shortly to pick you up. Its personnel are prepared to treat you with antibiotics, and our medical officer will be standing by to receive you aboard ship."

As soon as I had the captain's answer, I told

the four knights who were standing around
me to get behind some big trees close by at
the very edge of the woods. They did, trotting
away calmly but briskly. I got behind a thick
trunk not more than ten feet to one side of the
hut. About three minutes later, dad ran up.
He'd been listening on the cutter's radio, to
the police channel, and heard some traffic
between the corvette and the chasers.

"Their commanding officer is being careful," he said. "I don't think he's suspicious,
just cautious, but he's sending all three chasers down. Two will stand by out of sight, at
two thousand feet, watching everything on
infrascope. The corvette itself will be standing by at five miles.

"Now I'm going to talk to Arno," he added,
and hurried off into the woods.

So there went our plans, such as they were,
shot down. Instead of one chaser to deal with,
we had three plus the corvette. But somehow
I wasn't scared or worried now. I was calm as
anything, with this feeling that it would all
work out just fine, just the opposite of the
way I'd felt a little earlier. I didn't say anything to the knights about what was happening because I didn't have anything useful to
tell them. We'd just have to start out as if
nothing had changed, and play it by ear.

It took about ten minutes for the first chaser
to appear. I didn't see it coming because it
was dark, without even any moonlight, and
the chasers weren't showing any lights. One
minute there was nothing, and suddenly there
was this spotlight beam, dead on the front of
the hut. Then the chaser settled to the ground

no more than a hundred feet away, its spotlight still on. For a minute, nothing more
happened.

I avoided looking at the light, but it occurred to me that my four bowmen were probably staring right at it, because they'd never
seen anything like it before. It would make
their pupils contract, and they wouldn't be
able to hit anything in the dark with their
arrows.

So it was going to be up to me.

And if my guys started shooting blind and
missing when the agents were still outside
stunner range, I'd have to use my blaster instead of my stunner. And that would bring on
a violent response. They might shoot the whole
place up, and that would be that. *Well*, I
thought, *I'll just have to play it by ear—do the
best I can, and hope it works out.* I couldn't
very well yell to my men. That would tell the
political police that I wasn't alone down there.

I stopped thinking about anything and just
watched. The chaser was some light color,
maybe an off-white, and I could see the side
panel swing up and two guys come out. I
didn't know if there was a third man still
inside or not. One of the two had a hand up to
his mouth. It had to be holding a police band
communicator, because I could hear him talking as they walked toward us, although I
couldn't hear what he was saying. The other
man had a rifle in his hand, probably a heavy
military weapon.

They were just getting into good broad-beam
stunner range when I heard two bowstrings
twang, almost at once. Before I could react,

both agents fell; they should have been wearing some of that primitive chain mail. I guess my knights had looked away from the spotlight quickly enough; they could still see all right.

As soon as the agents fell, I sprinted toward their chaser, shouting "stay back!" to my bowmen as I ran. I didn't look to see if they were staying back, I just kept my eyes glued to the chaser door, running hard, ready to shoot if anyone showed there. I didn't even look to see if either of the downed agents was moving as I ran past them. It took me about four seconds to get there and jump in, and it was empty. Their radio was on, and a voice was saying, "Okay, MC-1, get clear of our firepower."

Maybe they hadn't been watching as closely as they should have. Maybe, seeing me running on infrascope, they thought I was one of theirs. Or maybe they'd gotten rattled when they saw their men go down. Anyway, I couldn't fly that thing on short notice; I'd need time to look it over and find out how.

But short notice was what they'd just given me. So I jumped back out and sprinted back to the trees, taking maybe five seconds for the return trip because I bent to snatch up the rifle laying by one of the fallen agents.

I just had time to give it to one of the knights when both other chasers arrived, hovering twenty or thirty feet above the meadow. I didn't know whether they'd seen me run for cover or not. Their spotlights flashed on, searching the edge of the meadow and the fringe of the woods. I huddled behind the knight's tree, giving him a ten-second course in the use of a blast rifle, then darted to my own tree as the beam moved someplace else.

From there, peering out, I aimed at one of the searchlights, and at almost the instant I fired, the knight shot out the other light, a split second ahead of mine. I shouldn't have been surprised, I guess. The knights had been smart enough not to let themselves be blinded, and it was obviously good sense to kill the lights if we could. But to use a totally unfamiliar weapon like a blast rifle maybe twenty seconds after he first touched one, and hit the target ... I'd heard dad say once that there was no explaining ability sometimes. Now I knew what he meant.

The only problem was that about one second later the guy shot out the spotlight in the abandoned chaser, too. I'd have preferred to keep its light intact.

Lights or not, after two or three seconds to get over their surprise, the two chasers started firing into the woods. But only for a moment. I later found out that the commanding officer on the corvette had started yelling at them over the radio to cease fire, that he wanted Klentis kel Deroop alive.

But at that time I didn't know that. I just knew that the shooting had stopped. Then everything was quiet for a little while, until after four or five minutes the corvette itself settled down and parked about fifteen feet above the ground. It was a half ovoid, with the flat side on the bottom, and it looked about a hundred and twenty feet long. I could dimly see turrets on it whose firepower could probably blow the hut away and tear trees into slivers.

It was interesting that the corvette's captain wasn't willing yet to risk his spotlights.

Then someone, probably their captain, called out on the loud-hailer. "Klentis kel Deroop! Come out and give yourself up. We know your family is with you. Give up or we'll destroy you all!"

My voice sounds a lot like my dad's, especially over a communicator. The trick was to talk like him—say the things he might say, using the words he might use, in case someone there had known him.

"That won't do you any good," I said into my communicator. "You weren't sent out here to kill me. The government wants a show trial.

"Now I've got something you want—me. And you have something to trade for me—my daughter. If you let her go—if you let her come out here into the forest to her mother and brother—I'll give myself up to you. What do you say to that?"

"I'm afraid not, kel Deroop," the loud-hailer answered. "Not in that sequence, certainly. But I will make you a counteroffer. First of all, I do prefer to take you alive. You are right about that, although dead will do. If you give yourself up, then, when we have you in our hands, we will release your daughter alive and well. If you do *not*, then we will throw her dead body from the ship and blast all three of you into small pieces.

"So what you must do now is come out of the hut with your hands in the air and lie face down on the ground, spread-eagled." He paused. "You have exactly one minute to make up your mind and do it."

One minute!

There was a door in the back of the hut and, crouched over, I darted to it and into the blacker darkness inside. My tree was only ten feet from the hut, and there was a pile of firewood between them that I ducked behind, so it seemed like there was a good chance they hadn't seen me.

The herdsman was still there. I could make him out dimly, a dark something, in the starlight that came through the doors. "You!" I said. "If you want to live, go to the front door and stop there."

Slowly he went.

"Now get down on your hands and knees and crawl outside, about thirty feet out. Then stop."

Peeking around the doorjamb, I watched him do it. I could almost feel his heart thudding in his chest, his breath nearly suffocating him. When he stopped, I said after him, "Now lie down on your belly with your arms and legs spread out."

So far, so good, I thought, as I watched him do that, too. Then, out of the dark sky, one of the chasers moved in, stopped to float a few yards from the herdsman, and its panel opened. I saw a hand and arm come out, and realized they'd just zapped the poor guy.

Quickly then it landed, and two men jumped out to load the body in. I fired my own stunner, set on wide beam and at maximum intensity. On wide beam, I couldn't miss, yet the range was close enough that they'd either be dead or out for hours. As soon as they fell, I turned and sprinted, running low, out the back door and into the woods behind, as hard as I could run, hooking left when I had a bunch of trees between me and the ship. I hadn't more than gotten out of the line of fire when the third chaser began to pump blaster charges into the hut. Chunks of wood flew around, and when the shooting stopped ten seconds later, the front of the hut was burning. Not burning very hard because it was pretty waterlogged, but putting out a lot of smoke.

By that time I was behind a big tree again, back in the woods a little way. About sixty or seventy feet in front of me I could see a Norman crouched behind his tree—the knight who had the rifle. I wondered what he thought of all that heavy-caliber shooting. Was he scared? My heart was pounding like crazy, and it mostly wasn't from running.

I started forward, bent low and trying to keep his tree between me and the infrascope head on the corvette, the problem there being that I didn't know where the infrascope head was. "It's me," I whispered as I approached the knight. He gave a quick glance back and then turned toward the meadow again. The corvette was moving closer, sideways, and I could see her turrets pivot, her blaster cannon swinging toward us.

I decided it was time to talk again, quickly, and reached for my communicator. But before I had it off my belt, I heard dad's voice from it. I could also hear him live, off to my right, and looked in that direction. He'd left the cutter and was behind a tree.

"Captain," he was saying, "you're making things too complicated. Let's look at this rationally. You don't trust me, and I don't trust you. We need to make the exchange a small step at a time, so that neither of us commits himself more than the other."

He stopped then until the captain's voice boomed out on the loud-hailer. "Continue!"

"First, have the other chaser land out in the middle of the meadow, where I don't have to worry about it. Then I'll come out into the edge of the meadow where you can see me. After that we can talk about the next step."

It seemed to me that if I were the corvette captain, I'd go along with that. I stared hard into the night, scanning around, not knowing where the third chaser was any longer. After maybe half a minute I saw it settle to the ground, way out near the middle of the meadow.

I wasn't sure whether I was supposed to go out now, or if dad was going to. He answered that by coming out from behind his tree to just in front of it, where he stopped.

"Next," he said, "your chaser crew will have to come out and walk at least one hundred feet away from their craft, in this direction, so I can see them."

The answer was quick. "Kel Deroop, I'm losing patience with you. You have already done something to four of my men—probably killed them. I am not having this crew step outside."

"Captain," dad answered, "I don't know what trickery you're up to, but I do know that a man short on patience would never have risen to your rank in the political police. And so far as your four men down here are concerned, they will wake up. I hope the same is true of my son, whom one of your men used a stunner on a few minutes ago.

"Now, I am not going out any farther while your chaser is in a position to rush me. Your chaser crew will simply have to come out and walk at least one hundred feet in this direction."

There was a long pause, maybe fifteen or twenty seconds. Then the loud-hailer spoke again. "Kel Deroop, I now have my turrets trained on the two derelict chasers near you. Should either of them move, or should any of you try to approach them, I will fire on them instantly. So if that is your plan, be advised that it is suicide to try. As for the other chaser, I will agree only to have her crew stand outside her door."

"Make it fifty feet, captain," dad said. "If they come out fifty feet, I'll come out fifty feet and we'll talk again."

A few seconds later the chaser opened, and its two men got out and walked a little way in our direction. They were about two hundred yards from us, so I didn't pay much attention to them. I was watching the corvette, my rifle gripped tightly in sweaty hands. Dad walked out about fifty feet farther.

Then I heard his voice again from my communicator. "Now it's your turn again. Land your corvette three hundred feet in front of me, open the gangway, and let me see my daughter."

Nothing visible happened for a while. The greepers caught a part of my awareness again, and the stars glittering in the black sky. Tiny biting insects I'd half noticed earlier hummed around my head, and absently I slapped at one and then another. I was amazed, in a detached kind of way, at how calm I felt. And not long before, I'd felt ready to come apart with nerves.

After a couple of minutes, the corvette lowered to the ground about three hundred feet away. Half a minute later a square of light appeared low in her side as the gangway opened. I could see three people standing in it, but couldn't tell who they were.

"Have her call out to me," dad told the captain, "so I know it's her."

A few seconds later I heard one of them shout. "Hi, dad! It's me, Deneen!" And it was; there wasn't any question about it.

"All right, captain," dad said into his communicator, "We've made start. But before we go any further with this, there is something you need to know, just in case you have some trick in mind. I am quite willing to stay on this planet; I can be successful on any inhabited world. You know my reputation. Now, the only reason I called you in is to get my daughter free. She has her whole life ahead of her, while I've used up the best half of mine. More than half. But if at any time you fail to carry out in this procedure, I'm going to break and run for it.

"Next, make sure she can hear me on her guards' communicators. Because if she doesn't follow my instructions, I'll assume she either didn't hear them, or she was prevented from carrying them out. Whichever, I'll cancel the whole thing. Then, when you get home, you'll have to report that you blew it. You'll never be able to cover it; it's sure to leak: You had me for the taking and you blew it."

He stopped and waited for half a minute, I supposed to give the captain time to give orders about the communicators. I wondered what dad's reputation was that the captain was supposed to be impressed with it.

"All right," dad said, "now I'll come out another twenty feet. That will put me roughly seventy feet from the woods. Then she comes out seventy toward me from your ship."

Without waiting for an answer, he took about eight steps in their direction, then stopped. Deneen came out about sixty or seventy feet, I suppose, with a guard on each side holding her arms. And then the thought hit me that what dad was doing was working, and we'd have Deneen back, and the corvette would have dad and take off, leaving us sitting here in the middle of a bunch of angry Normans.

My insides snapped into a hard, tight knot, even though I knew that was nonsense. I knew my father better than that; he had something else in mind. My stomach relaxed a little.

"That's far enough for her guards," he said into his communicator. "She comes alone from there, about halfway to me. That's still within their maximum stunner range. Then she'll stop; if she doesn't, they can zap her from where they stand. When she's stopped, I'll go most of the way to meet her.

"After that, she comes on slowly, step by step. And your men follow her step by step, keeping her within maximum stunner range.

When she's four or five steps from me, she runs for the woods. Understand? She runs for the woods *and they let her*. Then your men can zap me if they want, or they can just walk up and take me. Your choice."

Even I didn't believe that, and he was my father. Both he and the captain had tricks in mind, I was sure of it, and so were they. It was a question of whose trick worked.

"You either agree right now," dad went on, "or I head back for the woods. And remember, back on Morn Gebleu they want me alive. Your career is on the line."

I thought I knew the captain's trick. Back in imperial days, one of the things that emperors were known to do was root out whole families—leave no survivors. If the captain could get dad in his hands alive, he might blast every living thing in the vicinity, and report that he'd wiped out the kel Deroop family.

"You overrate your importance," the loud-hailer answered. "But all right, I'm quite willing. We really aren't interested in your family, you know, except as bargaining units. You're the one we were sent for."

At that moment I heard a terrible scream, and a second, from the direction of the chaser. Even as I jerked my head around to look, out of the corner of my eye I saw dad break into a sprint toward Deneen and her guards. At that same moment, Deneen did something—I couldn't see what, but it had to be hand-foot art—and one of her guards went down. Then she dove for the ground. An instant later dad and the second guard both staggered and fell, as if they'd stunned each other.

While that was in the middle of happening, I heard another wild yell, this time from the ship. I threw a quick glance that way, just in time to see two wolves disappear into the gangway. At that moment a trumpet blared a little way off to my right, and a couple of seconds later, a bunch of yelling and a wild scream came over my communicator. While that was going on, Arno's cavalry charged out of the forest.

I stood there confused for a moment, then realized that the nearby knights—my bowmen—were running on foot after the horsemen, toward the corvette, to get in on the action. I took off running toward dad and Deneen.

She was on her feet before I got there, and meanwhile, the knights were pouring into the gangway. When I reached dad, Deneen had already gotten the stunner from the zapped guard and used it on the other one—the one she'd laid out. Next, she gave the first zapped guard a second jolt, because dad had only gotten him at near-maximum range. She wanted to make sure he stayed out of action as long as necessary. Then, together, she and I dragged dad to the woods.

He wasn't unconscious; his body just wouldn't do what he told it to. I left him under the trees with Deneen, then ran as hard as I could out toward the middle of the meadow where the third chaser was. My rifle was ready in my hands, but I didn't need it; thirty or forty feet from the chaser, I found its two crewmen sprawled in the grass. Wolves had jumped them—several wolves, apparently—knocked them down and killed them almost before they knew what was happening. They hadn't even had time to use their blasters.

I took their weapons and got in the chaser, closing the door behind me. The panel light was enough to show me that the controls didn't look very much different from the cutter's. It didn't have a deep-space drive, of course, but all I wanted was to be able to use it to support the knights if I needed to. The radio was on, but dead quiet for the moment, only its dial light showing life. After locating key controls and instruments, I activated the drive.

I wasn't sure what to do next because I didn't know what the situation was on the corvette. I'd just decided to lift a dozen feet, and was reaching for the control stick, when a wolfish face caught my eye, looking in at me through the window. It was Bubba, so I pushed the switch marked *door*.

He jumped in and I closed the door behind him. Then he told me what had happened. When the corvette and all three chasers had arrived, dad had thought a message to him. When dad gave the signal, mentally, of course, the wolves would sneak out into the middle of the meadow from the far side. He would give the signal only in a situation where neither the corvette nor a chaser would be monitoring out there with an infrascope.

And, of course, both the corvette and the last chaser had ended up on the ground, with their attention on dad and the edge of the woods.

The really tough thing for dad had been

that he could only think instructions to Bubba. Not being telepathic himself, naturally, he couldn't get any feedback. He couldn't know whether Bubba and his pack were able to carry out his instructions, although he had a lot of faith in Bubba. He couldn't even know for certain that Bubba had gotten the message.

Dad has not only got guts; he's also smart and quick. He'd worked the whole thing out on the spur of the moment, after the corvette commander had spoiled our plans by bringing his entire command down. It also turned out that before dad came up to the meadow, he'd had Arno move his troops off to the west a little, so they wouldn't trample us when they charged.

Arno was to signal an immediate charge, the minute the wolves went into the corvette. And the knights would have to be quick because, while the wolves should have a big shock effect, it probably wouldn't last long. Especially if they ran into someone with a stunner or blast pistol in his hand.

The way it turned out, though, the wolves got to the bridge without casualties. Three of the local wolves, plus Bubba, had boarded the corvette, and the crewmen in the gangway area and corridor had freaked and run. The man in charge of the gangway had a stunner, but didn't have a chance to use it before he was knocked down and killed. Bubba didn't say who'd done it, but I could see blood on his muzzle.

The people on the bridge—there'd been four of them—had heard the yelling but had no idea what it was about. One of them had

drawn a stunner and killed the first wolf in—
Biggest. But Biggest's momentum had knocked
the man down. Then Blondie had grabbed the
guy's wrist. That took care of the stunner.
Slim had followed and gone for the throat,
which finished the guy off.

Meanwhile, one of the people hit the emergency door release and the rest of them piled
out, with Slim and Blondie after them. Bubba
had stayed until after he'd heard the Normans coming into the ship. When one of them
appeared from the corridor, sword in hand,
Bubba had jumped out, too.

While Bubba was describing all that to me,
I lifted a little way, flew over by the hut, and
landed. Bubba was pretty certain there weren't
any Federation people running around loose.
But before I left the chaser unattended, I took
the weapons out, and then the power activa-
tion plate, just in case. Then I did the same
for the other two chasers.

Meanwhile, Deneen and mom had brought
up the cutter and loaded dad into it. Dad's
mind was working all right, even if his arms
and legs weren't, and he could talk in an un-
derstandable mumble. He was giving the orders, and that was fine with me. I hadn't been
doing so badly, for a novice, but if this was an
example of how he'd operated as a revolutionary, I could see why the political police wanted
him so badly.

The Normans held the surviving Federation
people prisoner; they'd need them to help operate the corvette. But dad didn't trust the
political police, even as captives. So he told
me to go over with my stunner and make sure

they were all asleep and that they'd stay that
way the rest of the night. He even told me just
how to set my stunner. After I'd zapped them,
I was to find out from the ship's computer
how to disable the astrogational system, and
then do it. If I had any trouble with it, I was
to get him to the corvette and he'd see what
he could do. That was to keep the corvette
effectively tied to the vicinity of Fanglith.

It didn't turn out to be too hard. First I had
to access and follow parts A and B in the
control system's overhaul instructions. Then I
went to the engineering section, pulled two
flow plates, and ran them through the materi-
als recycler.

While I was at it, I also checked out the
firing code to make sure no one could operate
the turret guns without some instructions. I
didn't want the Normans shooting up the
woods before we left.

Then I went to the hangar and checked out
our old cutter—the one Deneen and I had
come to Fanglith in. I checked with mom on
my communicator, and she said to disable it.
We didn't want to leave the crew any way to
get back to civilization. That was no problem.
I just took the master cube out of the computer and put it in my pocket. The ones from
the chasers wouldn't fit.

The prisoners were no problem. The Normans had run amuck and only taken nine of
them. One of the crew had killed several
knights with a blast pistol and really trig-
gered a Norman bloodlust. There were federation bodies all over the place, and the decks
were gummy with their blood. There was no

way to get around without walking in it, of course, and when I got back outside, I almost wore my shoes out rubbing them in the grass, trying to wipe the blood off.

Back at the cutter, I hadn't had a chance to go to bed yet when Arno came over and asked me to bring the chasers on board the corvette. He was worried that Roland's men would go out and take them over.

He was already having trouble with Roland, who was claiming that he should be the head man now. The corvette was on his fief, he said, and therefore belonged to him. But more than half the Normans owed fealty to Arno and weren't ready to buy Roland's argument yet, even though it had a certain legal justification, I suppose.

An important factor was that Arno had their only blast pistol, and one of his men had their only blast rifle, though Roland's men had two of the four stunners they'd gotten their hands on. The Normans hadn't recognized the small-arms locker yet, and couldn't open it anyway until their prisoners woke up.

Arno didn't seem upset about Roland at all, though. I'm sure he'd expected something like this to happen. Born and raised a Norman, I suppose he'd have been surprised if it hadn't.

I wasn't eager to go into a situation like that. Roland's people might look at me as a promising hostage, or just covet my weapons. But Arno's guys would be there to protect me, and I thought we owed it to Arno to do it for him. Dad said fine, it was my option. Deneen said she wanted to go with me and back me up, and to my surprise, dad said all right and gave her his blast pistol! Mom never turned a hair.

None of us mentioned to Arno the weapons I'd brought aboard from the chasers. It just didn't seem like a good idea to bring it up. Without even saying anything to one another, it occurred to all of us that any more high-powered weapons among a group of squabbling Normans just wasn't a good idea.

Nothing happened when Deneen and I went back over to the corvette. I opened the hangar door and took in the three chasers, and then we came back to the cutter.

The family was all together now, and we could have left right then. We could have been on our way outsystem without even saying goodbye. But somehow, we decided to stay until daylight. We all felt a certain loyalty to Arno, even though one, we still didn't trust him, and two, we'd already set him up with the corvette, just as we'd promised. We all felt uncomfortable about leaving before he'd firmly established himself as boss over there. So I lifted to seven feet, where we were out of reach, and parked. Then we set up a watch schedule and I went to bed.

SEVENTEEN

I was on watch, and it still wasn't daylight, when I caught sight of someone walking across the meadow toward us. It was Arno again, and he wanted in. Bubba assured me that there was no one else around, and that Arno didn't have any treachery in mind at the moment.

So I woke up dad, who put on his jumpsuit and clipped on his stunner. Then I lowered the cutter and let Arno aboard.

All he wanted was to learn Standard from the computer. Knowing Standard would be a big advantage to him because then he could talk with the prisoners when they woke up, and he'd be the only Norman who could. And he knew that the computer was what we'd used to learn his language, so he figured it could teach him ours.

I lifted to ten feet, and Dad adjusted the learning program so it would teach Evdashian from the Provençal/Norman mixture we had in the computer. Evdashian was close enough to Standard that the prisoners would understand it.

Arno sat in one of the seats with a learning program skullcap on his head, while dad adjusted its controls. I sat back with my stunner on my lap and music on my headset to keep an eye on Arno. Bubba was there to catch any evil intentions that might surface.

Our distrust didn't seem to bother Arno a bit. Maybe Normans are used to things like that. Meanwhile, I was feeling good about this. Standard would give Arno the added advantage he needed. We could leave by midmorning, with no bad feelings.

Pretty soon it started to get daylight, and after a while the sun came up. Mom got up and started breakfast, and then Deneen got up, and dad again. Arno just sat there with his eyes half shut, absorbing words and syntax.

Suddenly my eyes bugged out; the corvette was lifting! I yelled and pointed. Arno snatched off the skullcap and stared, half crouched as if he were going to leap after them.

Abruptly it surged on a low trajectory course westward. The last thing I noticed was that the gangway and the emergency door to the bridge were both still wide open on it. I called a warning and took off after them on a higher trajectory.

Dad's first thought was that one of the prisoners had gotten free and made it to the bridge. But I told him about the emergency door, and the piloting was terrible, so we decided that one of the Normans had started fooling around at the control console. They were doing about five hundred miles an hour when they passed out over the ocean.

"What do you think's going to happen next?" I asked dad.

He never answered. He didn't need to, because right then it happened: The corvette exploded! It was a terrific blast that tore it completely apart. It even jarred the cutter, which was more than half a mile above and behind.

I didn't have to ask, or guess, what had caused it. I was sure she hadn't carried explosives that could have done that. No, whoever had been flying her had pushed the wrong switch, and she'd tried to go into faster-than-light mode—within five miles of a planetary surface! It wouldn't have been safe to try that at half a million miles.

We circled, and watched in the viewer as pieces of corvette splashed into the water far below. Arno had his pistol half drawn when Deneen zapped him. We had the only flying craft on Fanglith now, his last chance at an empire. He'd realized that, but she'd outdrawn him.

Her stunner had been set on low, though—customary when clipped on your belt—so Arno wasn't unconscious, just helpless.

Then we had some talking to do. First, I explained to Arno, in a general way, what had happened to the corvette. After that, dad asked him where he wanted to be put down. Arno mumbled that he didn't want to be put down.

If he couldn't have a sky ship, then he wanted to go to our country with us. He would swear fealty to us as our obedient vassal forever, so that we'd never have to worry about his trying to kill us or take over the cutter.

I felt really bad for Arno, and told dad I'd agree to his request. But dad said no. He didn't think Arno could survive or be remotely happy in a civilized world.

He explained to Arno just where our country really was—a world that circled a star so far away that you couldn't see it from here. The idea was totally strange to Arno, of course, but he seemed to get the general idea. And while he wasn't able to show much facial expression, zapped as he was, as far as I could tell by watching his eyes, it didn't shock him.

Arno really adjusted to facts very well. The problem was the adjustment of attitudes. He was a barbarian. The thing that made me feel so bad was that he was such a darn likable barbarian. And also, his dissatisfaction with Fanglith had grown out of his contact with us.

Dad pointed out to him that we'd kept our part of the bargain: We'd helped him get a sky ship of his own. He just hadn't been able to keep it, through no fault of his own or of ours.

Then an idea came to me. "Arno," I said, "when I met you, you were going to buy some warhorses, right? And take them to Italy or Sicily or somewhere where they were hard to get, and sell them to the Normans there for a lot of gold. Well, I know where there are more than thirty warhorses, and their owners will never be able to claim them now."

When he could move around some again, we put Arno down in the meadow in front of the hut. Then, from a couple of miles up, we watched him, mounted on Hrolf, round up the other horses and tether them in a string. It wasn't hard for him; Norman warhorses know a knight when they see and hear one, and do what they're told.

After that, he stripped off all their gear and put it in a pile. He'd have had a hard time explaining the saddles and so forth if he'd kept them.

We hadn't said anything about the little weapons stash we'd collected from the chasers. It just hadn't seemed like the right thing to do. But I'd given him a four-pack of recharges for his stunner and a belt magazine of energy cylinders for his blaster. I'd also explained to him that they wouldn't last forever— not long enough to make him King of Sicily. But surely they'd take him and his horse herd through any bandit gangs he ran into on his way to the Mediterranean.

The last thing we saw him do before he left, and before we kicked out of our parking coordinate, was hunt around in the meadow in front of the hut where the chasers had been. He was looking for any weapons that might have been dropped, I was sure. But we didn't see him pick anything up.

What he did have from our adventure together was the string of horses— probably as many as he could have bought. And he still had the purse of gold coins he'd come from Sicily with. That was a start on being a merchant, and with his intelligence and boldness, he might eventually end up buying and selling kings, or dukes at least.

I wished we could have said goodbye to the wolves. Their help had been vital to us, and they'd given it without asking anything in exchange. Bubba's wise eyes looked at me when I said it, his mouth grinning.

"Wolves all right," he said. "Have their own ways, their . . . values. Don't need thanks. They know what they did, and they tell it mentally for long time, to cubs and the cubs of cubs."

At a million miles, we shifted into FTL mode and headed outsystem. It had been a fantastic experience, and a successful one. We were together again, and Cookie was the only casualty.

I'd changed a lot on Fanglith; I wasn't the same kid any longer. Neither was Deneen, although she wasn't as put off as I was by the idea of going back to middle school again. I got used to it okay though, when we got back. But she and I agreed that we didn't want to stay on Evdash when we finished.

She and I talked it over quite a bit before we brought it up to our parents. We both agreed that we wanted them to train us so we could do something effective toward making the Federation safe and decent again.

They kind of smiled at each other, and dad said they'd been training us for that since we were born, just in case that's what we wanted to do. Now, he said, it looked as if it was about time for a new phase of training.

He hasn't said any more about it since then, and we haven't either, to him. But this morning before we left for school, mom told us not to make any plans for this evening—that dad was bringing home someone he was sure we'd want to talk with.

Deneen says that's it, that tonight is when we start the new phase. She's probably right. She usually is.

PATRICK TILLEY
CLOUD WARRIOR

"Reminiscent of Stephen King's *The Stand*." — *Fantasy Review*

"Technology, magic, sex and excitement. . .when the annual rite of selection for the Hugos and Nebulas comes around, CLOUD WARRIOR is a good bet to be among the top choices." — *San Diego Union*

"A real page-turner!" — *Publishers Weekly*

Two centuries after the holocaust, the survivors are ready to leave their underground fortress and repossess the Blue Sky World. Its inhabitants have other ideas....

352 pp. • $3.50

He was a new kind of soldier,
created for a new kind of war...

COBRA

TIMOTHY ZAHN

Hugo Award-winning author of *The Blackcollar*

The Cobras were a guerilla force of
cyborgs designed to die fighting in
the war against the Trofts – their
weapons surgically implanted, invisible
yet incredibly powerful. They were a
fighting force unmatched in human
history. But power brings temptation –
and could all the Cobras be trusted to
fight *only* for Earth?

352 pp. · $2.95

BAEN
BOOKS

VERNOR VINGE
THE PEACE WAR

55965-6 • 400 pp. • $3.50

BAEN BOOKS